VARSITY 170

Evan Jacobs

SADDLEBACK
EDUCATIONAL PUBLISHING

GRAVEL ROAD

Bi-Normal
Edge of Ready
Falling Out of Place
A Heart Like Ringo Starr *(verse)*
I'm Just Me
Otherwise *(verse)*
Screaming Quietly
Self. Destructed.
Teeny Little Grief Machines *(verse)*
2 Days
Unchained
Varsity 170

SADDLEBACK
EDUCATIONAL PUBLISHING
www.sdlback.com

ISBN-13: 978-1-62250-889-1
ISBN-10: 1-62250-889-0
eBook: 978-1-63078-018-0

Printed in Guangzhou, China
NOR/0115/CA21401969

19 18 17 16 15   1 2 3 4 5

Gravel Road™

DEDICATION

This book is dedicated to Mike Hartsfield, Dan O'Mahony, Gavin Oglesby, Chris Lohman, Colin Buis, Steve Itzkowitz, Jeff Caudill, Brian Balchack, and Dave Patterson.

Special thanks to Jeff Banks, Chris Nyhus, and the Beckman High School wrestling team for the technical advice.

Extra special thanks to Shawn Miller, who is an endless source of inspiration.

BEST FRIENDS

"You have Miss Scalf for English. Right?" Marcus's voice crackled a bit over Chad's earbud.

"Yeah, you do too. Right?" Chad turned the steering wheel into Marcus's tract.

The best friends were going to see each other in a few minutes. But they both saw no reason why they shouldn't be talking on the phone now. One of their favorite '80s songs, Journey's "Only the Young," was playing in the car through Chad's iPod. They often worked out to this song.

They first heard it in the movie *Vision Quest*. It was a wrestling movie, one of their favorites.

"Dude, I'm almost there. Don't make me wait," Chad said. He disconnected the call and cranked the music.

Chad Erickson and Marcus Pagel had been best friends since kindergarten. Today was the first day of their senior year. They had worked their entire lives for this moment. It was going to be the best year yet.

It had to be.

In nine months they were going to graduate. Marcus was headed to a four-year college. He didn't know where he was going yet: Stanford, UCLA, Washington. But wherever he went, he was going to wrestle. Chad wanted to go to a four-year school too. He had applied to Stanford and a few others. But he didn't think he would get in.

"I'm going to college," he would tell his girlfriend, Maria. "But I might have to go to a community college first."

There was still an outside chance that a scout from one of the Pac-12 colleges would see him. He'd be impressed with Chad. Scoop him up. Give him a full scholarship. Then Chad would wrestle for that school. And win.

That was Chad's dream since his sophomore year. But so far, it hadn't happened. Chad's parents didn't have a lot of money. Neither did Marcus's. Chad knew going to a four-year school right out of high school would be too expensive. Marcus didn't seem to care about the money.

He pulled up outside of Marcus's two-story home. Chad had practically grown up here. He was another son. Just one of the family. He could help himself to their food, or get himself a drink. Nobody would blink. Not even Marcus's little brother, Dave.

Chad sat there for a second. He thought about turning off his car and going inside.

But he didn't. Instead, he pressed a couple of buttons on his iPod and replayed "Only the Young" from the beginning. This way Marcus could listen to it too.

They weren't late. Yet. But if he went inside, Marcus would no doubt try to show him some YouTube video that Marcus and Dave found hilarious. Chad was an only child. He envied the relationship that Marcus had with his brother. Dave was a cool kid for an eighth grader. And he idolized Chad and Marcus.

"I'm gonna wrestle when I get to high school," Dave would say. "Just like you guys."

Suddenly, the red door to the Pagel house flew open. Marcus bounded outside. He had his backpack slung over his shoulder, a huge smile on his face. He was wearing dark jeans and a Shepard High School sweatshirt.

"Sup, sup!" he yelled across the driveway.

Chad smiled and waved to him. Marcus's mom and Dave appeared in the doorway. Chad could tell by Dave's smile that Marcus was probably teasing his mom before he walked out of the house.

"Marcus," she called in a hushed voice. "You're gonna wake up half the block!"

"Sorry, Mom!" Marcus hollered back. His mom's face dropped as he walked backward, looking at her. "I'm just saying hi to my boy. You and Dad always taught me to be a polite little boy!"

Dave started laughing even more, and this made Chad laugh too.

Then Marcus dropped to the ground.

Chapter 2

WORDS UNSPOKEN

Oh my God! Marcus!" his mom called.

But before she could rush over to him, Marcus hopped up. He was grinning from ear to ear. It had been a joke. Marcus was always messing around. Cracking jokes. Having fun. He wasn't mean about it. He always seemed to be going for a laugh. Even when he gave teachers a hard time, they didn't seem to mind. The cool ones responded in kind. This would egg Marcus on, but he did know there were boundaries.

"See you after practice!" Marcus got in Chad's car.

Chad waved at Marcus's mom so she didn't think they were being disrespectful. Dave was laughing hard. Marcus's mom started to scold him.

"Starting the day at second period was genius. Only having five classes is gonna be sweet," Marcus declared.

They had both set up their schedules to match, with fingers crossed that they would get the same teachers. But they didn't get every class together.

For the last three years, they loaded their schedules. Now that it was senior year, they wanted to take only five classes. It was actually just four classes because sixth period was physical education for varsity wrestling. Since they didn't start school until second period, they could stay up later and sleep in longer.

"I can't believe we're seniors," Chad stated.

"Yeah, it's awesome. We really gotta make this year sick. Totally blow it out." Marcus pulled a bottle of Coke out of his backpack.

"Maybe we should wait till we find out what colleges we're going to. In my case, what college I'm *not* going to."

"Don't be a such a stress case. You're going to a good school." Marcus took a sip of his soda.

Marcus always makes things seem so easy. How the heck does he do that? Chad wondered.

It was undeniable. Marcus was usually right about going with the flow.

"I hope."

"You will." Marcus stared out the windshield. There wasn't a hint of disbelief in his voice.

"How do you know this?" Chad smiled.

"Look, you're going to a good school. You wanna know why?"

"Why?"

"Because I say so." Marcus smiled.

Chad saw something in his eyes. It was confidence. It was going to be this way because Marcus said it would be. Chad needed to hear it.

Their senior year had just begun. One of the things Chad couldn't fathom—one of the things that Marcus never talked about—was what would happen when senior year was over.

What would happen when they were no longer together every day?

Chad knew there was no point in thinking about it right now.

"You're right," Chad said. "Senior year is going to be epic."

He pressed play on his iPod and "Only the Young" started yet again.

"Yeah! Old school. Love it." Marcus

tapped out the beat on his chest as the song blasted.

They fist-bumped like they always did and continued on to school.

Chapter 3

THE GIRLFRIENDS

Maria Tullai and Debbie Dowland greeted the guys as they made their way onto the Shepard campus. Maria had long brown hair and dark skin. She never used much makeup. Chad liked her fresh look. She always wore jeans or shorts, never dresses.

Debbie dressed the same as Maria. Some people thought they were sisters. Marcus was always asking her to wear tighter clothes. He would beg her to show more skin.

The couples made a tight foursome.

Maria wrapped her arms around Chad as they gave each other a warm hug. That was what Chad loved about hugging Maria. She made him feel like he was the most important person she knew.

Marcus and Debbie always made out in public. This morning was no exception. Chad wondered if it was something they did just because they could.

"Let's ditch school," Marcus suggested. "We'll go the beach."

"Yeah," Chad said. "Like that won't get us in trouble with Coach Mustain."

"We'll be back in time for wrestling practice." Marcus pulled Debbie closer to him and kissed her on the cheek.

"What am I gonna wear?" Debbie laughed. "I didn't bring my bathing suit."

"Well, I guess you won't wear one." Marcus leered at her.

"I think we should get to class before Marcus actually talks us into this," Maria said.

Maria was the most levelheaded person in the group. Chad liked that about her. They had been together for almost two years. She always kept him in check if he started worrying too much.

The group started walking through the campus. Students sat or stood, talking to one another or texting. Some girls used their phone cameras as mirrors to spruce up their hair or makeup.

There were Welcome Back posters everywhere. Clubs had also posted sign-up flyers for new members.

As the four of them walked together, once again, Chad couldn't believe their senior year was finally here.

"We rule this school, you guys," he said loudly.

Maria looked at him. Chad didn't normally say things like that. He left that kind of talk to Marcus.

"It's gonna be a great year," Maria added. "All of us together."

Chapter 4

ENGLISH CLASS

Chad and Marcus had English second period with Miss Scalf. It was their first class of the day. They liked the English teacher a lot. She had also taught their freshman English class.

Miss Scalf was the coolest teacher. She gave challenging assignments that really made you think. But she also did a lot of review. She made sure her students understood before moving on.

Some kids found this boring, but not Chad. He didn't always have the easiest time expressing himself. Miss Scalf's examples made it simpler for him to understand.

The teacher had also worked with him a lot as a freshman on how to write essays. How to use the proper MLA format. And all the other things that made English a difficult subject for him.

Miss Scalf went over the syllabus. Next she wanted the class to brainstorm a persuasive argument presentation. The project would be due in six weeks. The students could choose any topic to discuss. The whole class would judge how convincing they actually were.

She divided the class into groups of four students each.

"We need to come up with a great persuasive argument," Eliza Choi snapped at Marcus. "I don't suppose you have any ideas, do you?

"Let's make our persuasive argument

about a movie. *The Hangover*," Marcus suggested with a laugh.

Chad smiled and so did Joe Vasco. Chad didn't want to laugh and upset Eliza. He'd known her since sixth grade. She was a little high-strung, especially when it came to school. She never seemed to understand Marcus's sense of humor.

"We have to do it on something that's real." Eliza was starting to get mad.

"She said it could be a movie," Joe offered.

"What do you think, Chad?" Marcus asked. He loved doing that. Marcus knew Chad hated being put on the spot. That was why Marcus always did it.

"What would we say about it?" Chad asked.

At that moment, Miss Scalf came over to their group.

"How are we doing over here?" their

teacher asked. "I hear a lot of laughter." Miss Scalf smiled.

"Not from me." Eliza's tone was stern. Her arms were crossed.

"We can make an argument about why a movie is good. Right?" Chad asked. He had no problem talking to Miss Scalf. He couldn't always say that about most of his other teachers.

"Marcus wants to do our presentation about that nasty movie, *The Hangover*!" Eliza was hoping to sway Miss Scalf.

Chad and the others looked at the teacher.

"Choosing a movie is okay, and majority rules," Miss Scalf said as she laughed. "So you can do it. Are you guys going to try to convince people that it's worth watching? Or that it says something important about popular culture?"

"Yup, something like that." Marcus beamed.

"Sounds great!" she said. "Can't wait to hear it." Miss Scalf smiled and walked away. Marcus eyed Eliza with a triumphant smile. Eliza frowned. She knew Marcus had won. Like he always did.

Better just suck it up, Eliza. Marcus always rules, Chad thought.

Chapter 5

FOOD FOR THOUGHT

Chad and Marcus were walking to the parking lot. They ate lunch off campus. They'd been doing this since sophomore year. Freshmen had to stay at school. Being a senior made leaving for lunch especially cool.

"You know every time we do this," Marcus stated, "it's one of the last times."

"Isn't it always like that?" Chad asked.

"I guess I just now thought about it. We won't be doing this at the same time next year."

I know we won't. But why are you

bringing it up today? It's the first day of our senior year, Chad thought to himself.

"The girls want us to meet them at Debbie's car. Okay?" Chad changed the subject.

"Yeah." Marcus took out his phone and began to text.

Then Shawn Miller walked up. He was the manager of the varsity wrestling squad. He was a nice guy. Chad thought he tried to suck up to Marcus too much.

"You guys ready?" he asked.

"Ready for what?" Marcus asked.

"I thought Coach Mustain told you at practice yesterday."

"What, Shawn?" Chad was starting to get annoyed. Shawn was one of those people who had trouble getting to the point.

"Coach Mustain is trying to spread out the team's strength this year. You know how you guys alternate for each other?

Well, you two are gonna wrestle off for your spot. The one who loses is gonna go into the next weight class."

"What?" Chad asked, stunned.

He and Marcus both wrestled at one hundred seventy pounds. But there was a weigh-in shortly before each meet. Whoever didn't make weight would wrestle either one class up or down. This was usually Marcus. Chad felt that one seventy was his best match weight. He was always on weight.

"That's what I heard Coach telling some of the other coaches. He wants it done from the varsity team all the way to frosh-soph."

Chad tuned out. Suddenly the first day of the best year of his life was starting to be the worst.

Chapter 6

ELSEWHERE

Dude," Marcus smiled as he stuffed some fries into his mouth. "Stop stressing. I'll tell Coach that I'll go up in weight."

"Come on." Chad eyed his untouched burger and fries. "There's no way Coach Mustain is going for that."

Chad picked up his soda. His mouth was dry from anxiety. The restaurant was packed with students from Shepard High School. Marcus and Chad were sitting in a booth with Debbie and Maria. They had been so engrossed in their own conversation they'd barely talked to their girlfriends.

"You're worried for nothing—"

"It's *not* nothing." Chad was trying to show Marcus that he was upset without totally losing it. "If I don't wrestle at one seventy, there's no way I can win going up. Remember what happened last year? Coach asked me to try it. I got annihilated by that guy from Guerin."

Guerin High School had the best wrestling program in the city. Shepard was a close second. But Guerin was known for being the best. Some of their wrestlers had won college scholarships, and a few had even competed in the Olympic Games.

"You were sick, remember?" Marcus finished his last bite of cheeseburger.

"Hey," Maria broke in with a smile. "We're here too, remember?"

"Yes you are!" Marcus smiled as he

grabbed Debbie while she was drinking her soda.

"Marcus, I'm gonna choke!" she whined.

They all laughed. The first day of *their* senior year was still going great.

As Chad stared at his food, he realized that his best year might already be over. Before it even started.

Chapter 7

REALITY

You guys will be thanking me when you have your first meet," Coach Mustain had said. He'd started team training a month before school began.

Chad normally loved being in the wrestling room. But he wasn't happy to be there now.

With the knowledge that he might be wrestling Marcus in the back of his mind, Chad couldn't concentrate. They'd already run laps. And they had completed a ten-station circuit, switching every sixty seconds.

This is just wasting time, Chad thought. *When is Coach going to have us wrestle off? There's no way I can move up. I'll be annihilated.*

Drills were next.

The front headlock defense drill was where one wrestler began in a front head-lock position. The defensive wrestler took control of his opponent's elbow, attempting to step to the outside as he pushed his partner's elbow across.

"A good wrestler controls his opponent all the time," Coach barked.

Next was a drill Coach called "Iranians." The defensive wrestler began on the mat. The offensive partner was standing. The offensive goal was to lift the opponent. The defensive goal was to evade the other's moves.

As usual, Chad and Marcus were working with each other. Chad was jumpy and tense. Marcus could tell something was off. Chad wasn't being as aggressive as usual.

"Dude, you can grab me harder around the neck!" Marcus was annoyed.

"I wanna save my energy," Chad said as they got back into position to shoot against one another. The goal was for one wrestler to "shoot" into the legs of the other wrestler and take him down.

"I shouldn't see guys in cradles!" Coach Mustain yelled. He was tall and stocky. Coach Mustain looked intimidating, but Chad found him approachable. He could really talk to him.

Coach made Chad feel relaxed. Even so, Chad hadn't expressed his concerns about wrestling Marcus. He knew if he harped on it too much, Coach Mustain would lecture him.

As they ran the drills, Chad noticed that nobody else seemed to be bothered by competing for spots. They practiced like normal. Some bragged about how much they could bench press. Others talked about UFC matches.

Some guys just sat on a small bench in front of the wrestlers' cubbies, waiting for their turn. Inside the cubbies were shoes, hoodies, singlets, sweats, headgear, and water bottles.

Chad tried to loosen up as he and Marcus practiced fighting off their backs. Basically, one of them started with his back on the mat. He had to try and fight his way up.

Chad eyed a poster that showed a wrestler pinning his opponent. There was a quote on it by Willa Cather. It read: There are some things you learn best in calm, and some in storm.

Is that true? Chad thought. *I hope the storm doesn't last too long.*

"So," Coach Mustain said as he told the varsity wrestling squad his plans for expanding the squad's strength. "You're gonna have to wrestle off, guys. If you lose, you go to the next weight class."

He eyed Chad after he said that. For a second, Chad thought the coach could read his mind.

"I want my spot, Coach!" Marcus held up his hand. Chad had a feeling Marcus might say that. He couldn't resist putting Chad in an uncomfortable situation.

"Okay, then it looks like Marcus and Chad will be the first to wrestle off for ownership of one seventy."

The other wrestlers cheered. They knew this would be a dogfight.

Chad glared at Marcus. Then he looked away.

Chad was pissed. He planned to use his anger against his best friend.

THROWDOWN

Chad was the first to shoot in. That seemed to take Marcus by surprise.

Marcus got low. Somehow, before Chad knew what was happening, Marcus got him in a headlock.

Chad had been in this position many times. Coach Mustain always stressed that it was good if somebody got you in a hold like that at the beginning of a match. It meant your opponent was going to exert a lot of energy.

"If you can remain calm," Coach Mustain had said, "and breathe, you can actually make your opponent overexert himself."

Chad did his best to stop Marcus from tightening his hold. He wedged his fingers in between Marcus's arm and neck. He also moved a bit so that Marcus would use up more energy.

Marcus did.

Chad remained calm. He was able to forget how nervous he had been about wrestling his best friend.

The worry was gone.

At that moment, Marcus Pagel wasn't his best friend. He was an opponent.

When the time was right, Chad turned his body. He angled himself and started to scoot counterclockwise away from Marcus. Marcus tried to maintain his dominant position.

Chad stopped. As Marcus tried to dominate, Chad pressed as hard as he could and pried Marcus's arm away from his neck. It wasn't much. But it was just enough for Chad to turn out, whip around, and get back on his feet.

Everyone cheered as Marcus and Chad circled each other again.

Chad watched Marcus panting. He recalled the few times during the summer that he had asked Marcus to run with him. Marcus flaked. Chad realized that he may not be the better wrestler, but he was in better shape.

They hand fought. A few times, Chad let Marcus hold his wrist a little longer than he should have. But he meant to do it. He knew Marcus was getting tired.

Marcus shot in. To Chad's surprise, Marcus took him to the mat once more.

Again, everybody cheered. They knew they were seeing the team's two best wres-tlers in action. Marcus tried to grab Chad's

leg as he put his arm around his neck.
Chad easily pushed away Marcus's hands
and got back to his feet. Marcus followed.

But he was a little too slow.

Chad shot in. Before Marcus knew
what was happening, Chad had grabbed
him by the legs. Marcus tried to get out of
the hold.

Chad wasn't going to let him.

Using every bit of strength in his
legs, he lifted Marcus off the ground and
slammed him on his back in the center of
the white circle on the wrestling mat.

"Time!" Coach Mustain yelled.
"Erickson is up."

Chad was ahead! He was going to
be in the dominant position when they
resumed.

Chad looked down at Marcus. He was
still on the mat and staring at the ceiling.
Chad thought about extending his hand to
help him up, but he didn't.

Just then Marcus stood up. "Told ya you had nothing to worry about," Marcus said.

They made eye contact.

Marcus smiled.

Chad wondered what he meant by that. He opened his mouth to ask—

But Marcus's eyes rolled back in his head. His body swayed. He collapsed to the mat.

Chapter 9

NOT HAPPENING

Everybody in the room laughed.

They all assumed Marcus was playing a joke, just like always.

Chad stared at him. Even though Marcus was almost facedown, Chad saw his eyelids flutter and then close.

There was a moment of silence as the laughter dwindled down to a few snickers.

"Clear the room!" Coach Mustain seemed to jump out of nowhere. "Shawn! Call nine-one-one. Then get the nurse."

Shawn rushed over to the phone as the wrestlers filed out. They didn't move with

any urgency. Almost as if they were waiting for Marcus to get up. He was supposed
to jump up and bust out laughing. He'd
be thrilled that he played a joke on the
whole team. Best of all? He'd have punked
Coach Mustain too.

But Chad was the only one who knew
this was no joke.

Chapter 10

INTENSIVE CARE UNIT

Chad sat next to Coach Mustain in the waiting room outside the ICU. Marcus's parents were sitting across from them. They weren't saying anything. They just peered through the small windows of the ICU doors. Chad couldn't think of anything to say to them. It was like these two people he had known his whole life—his second set of parents—were suddenly strangers.

There's nobody else on the squad who competes at one seventy. If Marcus is really hurt, he'll be out of action for a while. That means I'll wrestle at one seventy. God, stop it! Selfish jerk, Chad thought, clearing his mind.

Coach Mustain was texting and emailing on his phone. Every so often he'd gaze out the window. Marcus's dad kept wringing his hands. His mom looked pale. Chad was worried, but he wasn't going to start being scared until Coach Mustain looked nervous.

There were many other people in the waiting room. It was a refuge for shell-shocked families hoping to hear that someone was going to be okay. They were talking a little but not much more than Chad, Coach Mustain, and Marcus's parents were.

CNN was playing on a flat-screen TV that was hanging on the wall. Chad could barely take in what the anchor was saying.

"There he is," Marcus's father said, pointing toward Marcus's doctor as the

ICU's doors opened. Mr. and Mrs. Pagel approached the doctor, who had stepped out of the ICU and into the waiting room.

Chad started to get up, but Coach Mustain put his hand on Chad's arm.

"Let's give them a moment to find out about Marcus. They may only be allowing immediate family in to see him right now," he said.

Chad tried to read the doctor's expression. But he couldn't. Then Marcus's mother dropped to the floor. Marcus's dad caught her as he burst into tears.

Chad looked at Coach Mustain. The coach's expression scared him.

Marcus's parents were both in tears. Coach Mustain's eye welled up.

"He can't be gone. He can't be gone," Marcus's mom was saying through her sobs. The doctor said a few more words to the devastated parents. Chad couldn't make them out.

Chad looked through the glass windows of the ICU. Any minute now he expected Marcus to appear. He had to. Marcus Pagel was a practical joker. He'd fallen down a million times since Chad had known him. But he always got back up.

Except today.

Chapter 11

SHOCK

You remember that?" Coach Mustain asked as his car slowly moved through traffic toward Chad's house.

"Yeah," Chad said.

Actually, he had no idea what Coach Mustain was talking about. Chad was thinking about Marcus.

Marcus was dead.

He had overshadowed Chad his entire live. He was funnier. Smarter. Did everything better than Chad. That was why Chad had gone at him so hard in the wrestling room. He'd had enough.

That's why I killed him.

Chad blocked out that last thought. He couldn't believe half the things he was thinking.

"You're in shock, Chad," Coach Mustain said. "You're gonna need some time to process this. A lot of time."

Chad just stared at the road. It was the same road he'd driven with Marcus that morning.

Chapter 12

HOME

Chad's parents took turns hugging him and telling him how sorry they were. He stared at them. They looked like strangers. They hadn't come to the hospital. After Marcus was admitted, his parents called Chad's parents. They asked them to go to their house and look after Dave when he came home from school.

Chad's parents got another call after Marcus died. Marcus's aunt and uncle came over to relieve them and be with Dave. The Pagels wanted the Ericksons to be home when Chad got there.

"Oh no," Chad suddenly said. His parents looked at him, worried. "I need to get the car. I left it at school when I went with Coach Mustain to the hospital."

Chad moved like he was going to walk out the door. His dad stopped him.

"Chad, you don't need to go get the car," his mom said quietly.

"Yeah. We'll get it tomorrow," replied his dad.

"But I need it tomorrow for school. Marcus is gonna be bummed if I can't pick him up."

Chad realized what he'd said after the words were out.

I'm not gonna be picking Marcus up tomorrow. I won't be picking him up the next day either. I'm never gonna pick him up again.

Chad's parents continued to stare at him.

"Go and rest, Chad," said his father.

"I'll call Joe and have him drive me to get it."

Joe Nelson was Chad's father's best friend.

Chad didn't have a best friend anymore. He did everything he could to block that thought.

Chad walked down the hall of his modest one-story home. He could feel his parents staring at him. He was sure they wondered if their son was ever going to be the same.

Chapter 13

DARKNESS

Chad didn't bother turning on the lights. He just went in his room and sat on the bed. He lay back and put his head on the pillow. He still couldn't believe what had happened.

As he stared up at the ceiling, the moon cast shadows on the wall. Chad closed his eyes, hoping that might make everything all right.

The weirdest thing was every few minutes he'd forget about what happened to his best friend. Then Chad relived the terrible afternoon all over again.

He wanted to cry but he couldn't. He thought it might make him feel better.

"Well, how long do we wait before we tell him he needs to talk to somebody about this?" Chad heard his dad ask his mom.

Am I in trouble? I didn't mean to kill my best friend. But murder is murder.

He managed to stop thinking about it.

It was an accident, he kept telling himself.

Chad wished Marcus was there. He'd laugh and tell Chad he was worrying too much.

But he would never hear that laugh again.

Chapter 14

TRYING NOT
TO MISS A BEAT

Morning came. Chad barely slept. Every time he started to nod off, he'd wake himself up. Eventually, he got ready for school, grabbed his backpack, and went to the kitchen.

His parents were sitting at the table. His mom was eating an English muffin. His dad was sipping coffee and reading the morning paper.

Chad was glad they were doing this. They looked normal. The more normal things looked, the more they had a chance to actually be normal.

"You're not going to school today, are you?" his mom asked as Chad poured himself some orange juice.

"I think I should. I don't want to stay home." Chad drank his orange juice in one gulp.

"Take the car," his dad said, pointing to the keys that were hanging up. "We picked it up last night."

"Don't you need it? It's your day."

"I'll take your mom's car. She's not working today," his dad said.

"Thanks." Chad took the keys and made his way to the front door.

"We think you should talk to somebody—" his mom started.

"Bye." Chad was out the door before she could finish.

Chad kept telling himself that he didn't need to talk to anybody. He knew if he just got to school and back into his daily routine, he would be fine.

Chad went out of his way not to take the same route that he had taken with Marcus. He would pass Marcus's house. He didn't ever want to go that way again. He figured it would be like living in the past. Chad knew he couldn't do that. He had to keep moving forward.

No matter what.

Chapter 15

MIRROR BEHIND

Walking through the campus was a lot more difficult than Chad thought it was going to be.

It wasn't because he was sad or scared. It wasn't because the sun was so bright it hurt his eyes. And it wasn't because of all the signs for school clubs and upcoming events.

It was because of the stares. Everybody seemed to be looking at him without trying to *look* at him. It was awkward.

Maria walked up to him. She took his hand and looked up at his face.

"Hey," she said. "I can't believe it."

Chad could feel her looking at him. He met her gaze briefly. Normally he had no problem looking into her eyes. But nothing was normal today. Chad knew that things would never be normal again.

"I tried calling you yesterday. I was gonna come over, but … I didn't hear from you," Maria went on.

Chad looked away. He had nothing to say. He wasn't in the mood. He didn't want to be mean. He really didn't feel like talking.

"Let's do something today after school. We can meet after wrestling …" Maria caught herself.

They never saw each other after school. She was a member of the Associated Student Body. She was the senior class representative. She usually had meetings with other ASB members while he was in wrestling practice.

"Okay, call me." He walked away. If he had thought to say goodbye, he would have. But he wasn't thinking about anything except getting to class.

Miss Scalf's English class wasn't much better.

Again, everybody was trying not to look at him. He saw Eliza Choi glance his way a few times.

Even worse was seeing Marcus's empty desk. Chad quickly looked away. Its cheap wood, cold metal, and plastic blue chair looked abnormal, like it had been placed there for everybody to see. To let them know that they too could die at any moment.

Chad sat down and took his book and folder out of his backpack. The instant he looked up, he saw Miss Scalf in front of him.

"Hey," she said.

"Hi," Chad said. He looked down at

his desk. It looked even more colorless and plain today.

"If you want to skip today, I'm fine with it. Skip tomorrow too. I can't believe you're even here," Miss Scalf offered.

"It's okay."

Normally, Chad enjoyed talking with Miss Scalf. Now he just wished she'd leave him alone.

"If you want to talk—"

"Okay," Chad said tersely.

Miss Scalf smiled slightly at Chad, then went to the front of the class.

The bell rang.

Students were still standing up. Organizing their schedules with Miss Scalf. Basically ironing out the fact that school had just started after a long summer vacation.

Ever since sophomore year, he'd started taking school more seriously. As a result, he always felt the pressure to perform. To make good grades. And to be a top-notch wrestler.

Marcus helped him with that. He helped him with everything.

For the first time since yesterday, Chad realized Marcus wasn't there. He never would be again. A cold chill rushed through him. He started to get scared.

And sad.

"Chad." He looked up. Next to Miss Scalf was an office aide. A senior Chad didn't know.

Miss Scalf walked over to his desk as discreetly as possible. He felt like everybody in the classroom was looking at him. And they were.

"Principal Harris wants to see you. Is that okay?"

"Why?" Chad asked.

Am I in trouble? Is Principal Harris going to grill me about what happened?

"I think he just wants to talk to you. See how you're doing."

"I don't want to fall behind."

"You won't. I want you to go." Miss Scalf gave him a reassuring look.

Chad got up and did his best not to think about everybody staring at him.

He couldn't help eyeing Marcus's empty desk again as he left.

Chapter 16

HIS OWN GOOD

I need to wrestle," Chad stated as calmly as possible. "I *have* to wrestle."

Chad was doing everything he could to meet Principal Harris's gaze. He was also trying to talk in a tone that wasn't defiant.

Principal Harris sat across from him with both hands on his large desk. On it was his computer, many file folders, and a framed picture of his family. Behind his desk were photos of him mingling with students. There were also some awards and degrees on the walls.

The principal was being nice. He told

Chad how much he liked Marcus. How sad he was about what happened. How much the school was going to miss him.

"I think you need time to process this situation," Principal Harris stated. He wasn't being unkind. He seemed to be thinking about Chad's feelings.

"I can do that by wrestling."

"Have you talked with your parents at all about grief counseling?" Principal Harris sat back in his chair.

"A little." Chad stared at the floor. "I just don't want to fall behind. If I stay at home, all I'm gonna do is think about—"

Chad stopped himself before he said Marcus's name. It felt weird saying it. Like he was swearing in front of an adult.

"There are gonna be scouts at these meets. If I can impress one of them, maybe I can get a scholarship. That's not gonna happen being at home doing nothing."

Principal Harris stared at him for what seemed like a long time.

"Okay, but if you start having problems, or you need somebody to talk to, you know where I am. All right?"

"Yeah," Chad said.

He wanted to smile at Principal Harris. He wanted to thank him for caring about him.

But Chad didn't.

He didn't think he could do anything right now.

Chapter 17

BELLS

Normally the lunch bell would've been met with some excitement from Chad. He and Marcus, along with the girls, only had forty minutes to get their food and get back to school. Marcus loved to push it as much as he could.

Today the bells only symbolized how different things were. At snack time, Chad hid out in the library. He ate the granola bars and fruit his mother had packed that morning. He was used to eating off campus at lunch. He didn't bother bringing any more food.

Worse was the realization that he didn't have Marcus to eat lunch with. They had been eating lunch together since kindergarten. The only times they had missed was when one of them was sick, or if they'd had a stupid disagreement. And those never lasted long.

Chad wasn't going to be eating with Marcus ever again.

As he listlessly made his way through the crowd, he could feel the loss washing over him. He couldn't let the pain get too bad. If he did, he'd lose everything.

"Hey, let's go out." Maria wrapped her arms around his.

Chad looked at her. She looked like a stranger. He felt detached.

"Okay," he said, happy to be thinking about something else.

"So I was thinking we should have the Key Club event at the McBain Hotel. The problem is that it's too expensive." Maria took a sip of her soda.

"Oh."

They were eating at Hertz's Pizza Parlor. It was one of Marcus's favorite places. Marcus always got the same thing. Two slices of pepperoni pizza, a side salad, and a soda. He never ate the salad, so he'd give it to Debbie.

Today Chad and Maria got a slice of cheese pizza, a side salad, and a soda. The one bright spot in this awful day was that Chad had gotten his homework done in class. Because it was the second day of school, there wasn't much to do. He'd have nothing to keep himself busy when he got home. He wasn't sure if that was a good or a bad thing.

"Tanya and Kerry are being so catty. They want to have the event at Galloway's on the beach. That place is way more expensive than my suggestion." If

Maria was bummed by Chad's silence, she certainly wasn't showing it.

She continued talking. Chad turned his attention to the front door.

Just like in the hospital, he got lost in the idea that any second Marcus was going to walk in. This whole thing had just been an elaborate senior prank. It was Marcus's way of "blowing it out" as he said. Chad got so excited by the idea that he started to think it might be true. He started to wonder what else Marcus might have up his sleeve.

He'd been staring at the door for so long that Maria eventually waved her hand in front of his face.

"Chad!" Her tone was firm. She was probably at her limit with him right now. Chad knew she didn't like to be ignored.

He didn't care. At that moment, he couldn't help but glare at his girlfriend. For a brief second, he was happy thinking

that yesterday had all been a gag. Maria
had ruined the fantasy.

She didn't mean to, but Chad was
angry with her just the same.

Chapter 18

PRACTICE
MAKES IMPERFECT

Chad finished tying his shoes, shut his locker, and locked it. He was surprised how normal he felt putting on his sweats and hoodie before practice. These were the same clothes he'd worn yesterday. But it didn't bother him.

Chad noticed the clothes felt a little heavier today. He figured it was probably because he hadn't slept last night. He was looking forward to going home. Getting to his room. Lying on his bed. Tuning out the world.

He looked around the locker room. He saw a few basketball players but no wrestlers. What was going on? Did he miss practice?

It was only the second day of school.

He walked into the wrestling room and saw all the wrestlers—frosh-soph, junior varsity, and varsity—sitting on the floor in front of Coach Mustain. They all looked at him as he approached. They weren't trying to *not* look at him like everybody else. Chad didn't know which he liked less. He just knew he didn't like being looked at.

Nobody would say it, but Chad had done something wrong. He used too much force slamming Marcus on the mat. It had been an accident, but it was still wrong.

"No practice today, Chad," Coach Mustain said.

Chad noticed that Coach Mustain had tears in his eyes. And he wasn't bothering to wipe them away.

"We're just going to take the practice time to talk. Do you have anything you want to say?"

If all the eyes in the room hadn't been focused on Chad, they sure were now.

"No." His tone was low.

He sat behind everyone on the mat.

Chad wanted to get this over with. He wanted things to go back to normal. He'd give anything to have Marcus come walking through the door of the wrestling room.

Chad knew he wouldn't. He was dead.

And he blamed himself.

Chapter 19

DEPRESSION

After the wrestling meeting, Chad talked to Coach Mustain.

"Are we gonna practice this week?" Chad didn't want to seem indelicate. He was just clinging to something familiar and comfortable.

"Yeah, we'll be back at it tomorrow. I just wanted to take today …" Coach Mustain continued talking. Chad tuned him out. He wanted to get out of the wrestling room and go home.

Chad lay on his bed. He was watching

Reddit videos on his iPad. A kid was singing a One Direction song in a talent show. It was supposed to be funny. But Chad wasn't laughing. He knew Marcus would've loved it. It was the type of video that he would've texted to Chad just to bug him.

Chad wanted to get out of his room. But dinner that night had been uncomfortable. Normally, he and his parents would have a lively conversation. They would talk about their day or their weekend plans. Marcus also ate over a lot. He loved Mrs. Erickson's cooking, especially her meatloaf.

Tonight the conversation was forced. Stilted. On top of that, his parents brought up grief counseling again. His mom talked about how she'd spoken to Marcus's mom. Mrs. Pagel wanted to know if Chad wanted to say anything at the funeral, which was Sunday. Chad didn't respond.

He figured his startled expression probably told his mom the answer.

Chad went to his room without eating much.

As he stared at the screen of his iPad, he couldn't help but get a little angry. He just wanted to feel better. Even more than that, he wanted this whole thing with Marcus to slow down. The funeral. The grief. The acceptance. Chad wasn't ready for any of that.

Chapter 20

12 OUNCES OF COURAGE

Later that night, Chad went to get some-thing to eat. He thought he might be able to eat if he wasn't around his parents. His mom had put his food away. Chad pulled the plate out of the fridge. He wasn't going to heat it up.

Before he shut the door, he noticed his dad's beers. It reminded him of when he and Marcus were little kids. They would sneak a beer at a family party and drink it. They didn't do it because it tasted good. They did it because they knew they shouldn't. There were ten bottles of beer at the bottom of the fridge that nobody was in any particular hurry to drink.

Chad didn't really know why he did it. He pulled out a beer. He took that and the food and went back to his bedroom.

THE MOURNERS

Pastor Lohman stood in front of the congregation. The casket containing Marcus Pagel's body was open. Chad could see Marcus's partial profile from where he was sitting.

"Family and friends, it is moments like this that remind us just how precious the sanctity of life truly is."

Chad noticed that Pastor Lohman's words seemed to be affecting everybody at Marcus's funeral. There was a lot of nose blowing and soft crying.

Chad felt nothing. Empty.

He looked around. He realized that even people who weren't crying looked like they had been at some point.

Chad was sitting with his parents and Maria. They were directly behind Marcus's family. Marcus's mother and father were sobbing just as much as they had been at the hospital. Dave was crying too.

Chad still hadn't spoken with them. He'd hid out in the bathroom until the funeral service was about to start. Then he walked over to his parents and Maria. She took his hand in hers and squeezed it. He tried to squeeze it back. He even tried to smile.

"And though time may go on, we will never forget what a bright light Marcus was in all of our lives," Pastor Lohman continued.

As Chad watched him, he started to

get angry. He felt like Pastor Lohman was enjoying this. The more he thought about it, the angrier he got. Then suddenly he started to feel sad.

He quickly looked at the ground and closed his eyes.

Keep it together. This service will be over soon. Then I can go back to my room. It's the only place I feel comfortable.

When he opened his eyes, he saw Dave looking at him. Had Chad been quicker, he would've looked away.

Instead, Dave gave him a half-smile and a wave. Chad raised his head and looked down again.

Chad figured that Dave was just being nice, forcing that smile and wave at him. He knew Dave hated him deep down for killing Marcus, his idol. Chad knew Marcus's parents hated him too.

He knew everybody hated him. That

was fine with him. He figured he deserved it after what he did.

Chad didn't want to be around them anyway.

Chad stared at Marcus's dead body. He couldn't believe how calm his friend looked in the casket. The more Chad stared at his dead best friend's profile, the more it looked like he was smiling. Chad figured he probably was.

Marcus would never be down, not even at a funeral. Sure, he might put on a somber face. But he wouldn't let anybody be sad around him. He'd find a way to cheer them up. Marcus always did.

Chad started to think about the wrestling match again. He knew he'd wanted the one-seventy spot too much. He knew he shouldn't have taken it so seriously. He should have treated Marcus as his best friend, even in that important match.

He wasn't supposed to die. I just slammed him down a little harder than I meant to.

Chad snapped out of his musings. He knew he'd been staring at his best friend for too long.

He knew people would want him to get over it and move on.

Chapter 22

NOW WHAT?

Maria was saying something to Chad. He wasn't paying attention.

She was standing next to him. But he didn't hear a word she was saying. They were near the entry of Marcus's house. People were eating and talking, the way they might on any day at any party. Chad had gone out of his way not to listen to any conversations, but it was hard to tune out the low voices all of the time.

Adults were talking about their jobs. Younger people were talking about school.

Chad was thinking about Marcus's bedroom. It was upstairs at the end of the hall. On the door was a poster of Georges St-Pierre, the UFC Light Heavyweight Champion. He was Marcus's favorite fighter. Chad had liked Anderson Silva a lot until he started losing.

Chad wanted to go into Marcus's room. He wanted to shut the door and scream. He hated being in the Pagel home. He couldn't wait to get out of there.

"Should we do that?" Maria finished.

Chad looked at her. He started to get angry. He just wanted her and everybody else to leave him alone. The more empathy people showed to his perceived pain, the more upset he got.

"Maybe," Chad said. That was the best he could offer. He didn't know what Maria had said. He figured it was okay to be noncommittal.

Chad saw his dad talking to Coach

Mustain. He was probably saying that Chad needed help.

Then he saw Marcus's parents talking to Pastor Lohman. They were nodding their heads as they stared at him intently. Chad figured anything Pastor Lohman said would momentarily ease their grief. They were so devastated. Like Chad, they just wanted Marcus back. The only difference was Chad didn't think Pastor Lohman could help him.

He wanted to go into the backyard. But that's where most of the wrestling team was. Every so often Chad could hear them talking. They missed Marcus, but sometimes they forgot where they were. They'd get loud and laugh. Then they'd stop just as quickly as they started. They knew they'd gotten too happy.

Chad wanted to ask if Marcus was that hard to remember.

Later that night, Chad pulled a beer out

of the small refrigerator in his room. He had swiped another one from the kitchen the day before. He cracked it open and took a look drink.

He didn't know if he liked the taste of beer. He didn't know if the brand he was drinking was any good. He just knew it made him feel better. Less nervous. Less edgy. Less angry. And less able to feel.

And that was exactly what Chad wanted right now. To feel nothing.

Chapter 23

OVERWEIGHT

The scale eventually stopped at one hundred seventy-four pounds.

This was the heaviest Chad had been two days before a match. It was the first match of the year. He wasn't going to tell Coach Mustain or anybody else. He just needed to eat less and not drink any beer. Chad was going to miss the beers more than the food. They were making the days bearable.

Practice was going well. He had been really quick and strong. He didn't let himself get caught in any traps. He'd also fought off his back really well.

"Damn, Chad," Ryan Abad joked. "You been working out or something?"

Ryan wrestled one weight class below Chad.

"No, I've just been running." Chad wiped some sweat from his face.

Chad liked Ryan. They'd been friends since middle school. They hadn't really ever hung out much. Chad wondered if maybe now he would hang out with Ryan and his friends. They were mostly wrestlers, and they all liked Chad. Aside from Maria, he wasn't spending time with anybody.

He knew there was no replacing Marcus, though.

Coach Mustain asked Chad to stay after practice. Chad figured Coach had found out about his weight somehow. He started making up a story to cover himself.

"I'm not too sure you should wrestle at this first meet." Coach Mustain checked his phone as he spoke. He looked at the ground. He seemed to be having a hard time looking Chad in the eye.

"Coach! Did you see me today? I'm fine." Chad hoped he didn't sound whiny, but he *had* to wrestle at the first meet. He didn't know when a scout might be attending. He had to be perfect in all of them. "You don't have anybody to fill my spot!"

"Sure we do. There's—"

"Coach, you know nobody is as strong as me at one seventy." Chad's tone rose as he cut off Coach Mustain. Coach Mustain's eyes got wide, like he was getting angry, then his expression relaxed.

"You really think you're up for this?" Coach Mustain relented. "Dominic Vasquez is no joke."

Dominic Vasquez was a senior at Guerin High School. He had been wrestling at one sixty through his junior year. Nobody from Shepard High had ever beaten him. Over the summer he had a growth spurt and was now wrestling at one hundred seventy pounds.

"I'm up for this. Dominic's only been at one seventy for a few months. I've been here for two years."

Chapter 24

ALONE IN A CROWD

You're probably gonna get pinned as soon as the whistle blows!" Amman Owens yelled at Tighe Nishamura.

"At least I'm wrestling tonight!" Tighe shot back.

There was always this kind of teasing when the team drove to wrestling meets. It helped relieve the tension.

Surprisingly, Chad found himself laughing. He even made few callouts of his own, which got big laughs. He and Ryan sat together. The whole bus talked smack about their opponents. A victory party at Hertz's Pizza was planned. The owner liked them. He'd let them stay as long as they wanted. Provided that they didn't get too rowdy.

"Hey, Chad, you looking forward to pizza at Hertz's tonight? We can get our grub on after not eating to make weight."

"Yeah," Chad replied as he rested his head on the seat.

Then he got a weird feeling.

He was *enjoying* himself.

How could he do this? Marcus, his best friend, had died. Had Chad suddenly gotten over him? Maybe this was how life was?

People die. That's it.

Chad wondered how much time Ryan might have. He looked at Coach Mustain and wondered the same thing about him. Then Amman, Tighe, and some of the other members of the team. Chad thought about his parents. They were in their forties. How much longer would they be around?

What about Maria? Or me?

The jokes on the bus continued, but Chad wasn't participating anymore.

He'd stopped enjoying himself.

Chapter 25

OVER BEFORE IT STARTED

The moment he got to Guerin High School, Chad felt unsettled. He'd felt this way before most wrestling meets. But the feelings always subsided before. This uneasiness wasn't going anywhere. He knew it when he walked out to meet Dominic Vasquez inside the bright white circle on the mat.

He felt like his headgear was suffocating him. He had blurry vision. On top of that, his singlet felt too tight. He'd gained and lost four pounds. He'd passed the weigh in.

He and Dominic shook hands. Even that took effort. Chad's arms felt heavy. His legs felt like jelly as he walked. He got in a crouching position. That took even more out of him.

Chad wanted to tell Coach Mustain that something was wrong. He wanted to tell the referee too.

But he knew he couldn't. Like Marcus's death, Chad was just going to have to tough this one out alone. He figured he'd done okay so far.

The whistle blew.

Dominic Vasquez was five eight, but he looked a lot heavier than one hundred seventy pounds. He was very muscular. And he wore a look of determination that Chad knew he couldn't match.

Not on this night.

Before Chad knew what was happening, Dominic shot in and took him to the mat. Chad let out a small groan.

I can deal with this. I know what to do. Calm down. Stay calm. Breathe. Breathe.

The only problem was that Dominic didn't seem to have a problem maneuvering Chad on the mat. Chad tried to get away. But before he knew it, he was on his back.

I got this. I know how to fight off my back. I've done this a bunch of times, he told himself. *Argh*!

He'd spent a lot of time convincing people he knew what to do. He'd be fine wrestling Dominic Vasquez. But he hadn't really put together a plan on how to beat this fierce opponent.

Dominic wrapped his arms around Chad's neck and leg. Chad was in a hold that he had to get out of. He tried but he couldn't.

The referee slammed the mat once with his hand.

Chad did his best to wriggle free. But he couldn't even move.

The referee hit the mat again. One more hit and Chad was pinned.

He did his best to break free, but Dominic was just too strong.

"Ahh!" Chad screamed.

But he didn't go anywhere.

The referee slammed his hand onto the mat a third time.

Dominic let go. The match was over.

Chad looked at the clock. He had been pinned in less than ninety seconds.

Chapter 26

OUT

Chad sat alone in the locker room. His only solace was the fact that most of the wrestlers on Shepard's team had also lost.

None of them had been dominated like Chad, though. He was positive videos were already uploaded to YouTube. He was so upset. And humiliated. He didn't bother to shower. He threw off his headgear and put his sweats and hoodie back on.

Some of the other wrestlers still talked about going to Hertz's Pizza. But Chad had zero interest.

"Well," Coach Mustain said, smiling as

he walked over to him. "I hate to say I told you so."

"I think I lost too much weight too soon—"

"You've cut weight like that before." Coach Mustain abruptly cut him off. "Listen, Chad, have you talked with anybody about what happened? Maybe a professional? Someone on the outside."

"My head wasn't right," Chad protested. "I barely did any homework on this guy. Like Marcus and I used to. If he were here …"

Chad stopped talking. He didn't want to say too much about his dead best friend. If he did, he knew that would make it real. So far, he had done a good job of denying the truth.

"Chad." Coach Mustain's face and tone became very serious. "You need to get some help. Until you do, I'm not comfortable letting you remain on the team."

He stared at Coach Mustain.

He didn't know what was worse: being off the team or not having Marcus.

He wanted to kick himself the minute he had that thought.

Chad knew not having Marcus around was *way* worse. The problem was, now he didn't have wrestling either.

Chapter 27

THE LONG DRIVE HOME

Earlier, Chad had planned to ride home on the bus with his teammates. He had planned to go to Hertz's Pizza and celebrate their victory. He had planned to show everybody that he was back and better than ever.

Instead, Chad was sitting in the backseat of his dad's car. He was holding his iPod. Staring at the darkness of the road. Trying to focus on the light patterns flickering on the freeway. The back of the car was dark. Chad could feel himself getting lost in it.

And that was just fine with him. He didn't talk to his parents. He didn't tell them about Coach Mustain kicking him off the team.

"I'm not sure yet, but I'll probably be home then," his dad was saying.

"Okay. Well, let me know because they are expecting us at six thirty. I want to tell them if we're going to be late."

Chad couldn't believe their conversation. They had tried to console him about the match. He shrugged it off. When they saw that he wasn't talkative, they started talking about everyday things.

One thing they weren't talking about— nobody was talking about—was Marcus. He was all Chad thought about. He felt like everybody wanted to move on. They were all being too quick to forget about him.

Would I feel better if everything wasn't business as usual? They all seem to be over it. I'm so confused. I want to get past this, but I can't. I shouldn't. He was my best friend.

He put his earbuds in. Flipped the iPod to shuffle. And hoped the songs would take him away from everything and everyone.

Chapter 28

DATE NIGHT

Now, this isn't for sure. Dahlia and Christy said that we might be nominated for homecoming king and queen."

Chad could feel Maria staring at him after she said that. More than anything, he could sense her sadness at his non-reaction to her news.

"That's cool," he said.

This was their first real date in a couple weeks. Since everything had happened. Since Marcus. They were driving to Hertz's Pizza.

"You don't want to be homecoming

king?" Maria turned and looked out the front window.

"Sure I do. But we haven't been nominated for it yet."

Chad wanted to say that the only reason they were even being considered was because Marcus was gone. If he were still alive, Chad knew that he and Debbie would have a lock for a nomination. They'd probably win too.

"It is our senior year," she offered.

"Yeah." Chad knew that all too well.

He also knew that his apathy hurt Maria's feelings. He didn't want to do that.

"It'd be great." Chad tried to sound excited. He took Maria's hand in his. He hoped his hand didn't feel as listless as the rest of him did.

"You really think so?" Maria turned toward him again, beaming.

"Yeah," he said. His eyes stayed on the road ahead.

She squeezed his hand and leaned over to give him a kiss. Her lips were soft and warm. Chad felt like his were chapped and stiff.

"I don't really care about stuff like this. But we are seniors. We'll remember this experience forever." Maria continued talking. She squeezed his hand again as she did.

For a second Chad felt good.

He'd made Maria feel better, even though he felt awful.

Chapter 29

GONE AND FORGOTTEN

No you wouldn't," Maria said as she took a bite of her pizza.

"Of course I would." Chad laughed as he took a sip of his soda.

He and Maria were actually having a good time. Somehow he had convinced himself to forget about everything on his mind and just enjoy their date.

Hertz's Pizza was a special spot because it was where they had first gone when they started dating. Tonight, Chad had even made sure to order a pepperoni and sausage pizza. It came with a salad and breadsticks. This is what they had eaten on their first date.

"Would you really break up with me if I went to see One Direction?" Maria eyed him with happiness. It had been a while since he'd seen her eyes sparkle. It had been a while since anyone had looked at him with joy. Chad wondered if anybody realized how sick he was of being pitied.

"I think that's a breakupable offense." He grinned.

Chad couldn't believe how good he felt. He'd had a beer a few hours before their date, but he figured it had worn off by now.

He was happy he had money for the meal. His parents still gave him an allowance. Chad had worked part-time both his sophomore and junior year. He had to quit when work, his studies, and wrestling proved to be too much for him to handle.

Since he didn't have wrestling anymore, Chad thought he'd probably get a job again. He was nervous, though, because he wanted to get back on the team. He still had dreams. He wanted to go to college.

Chad and Maria continued to talk and flirt with each other. He wasn't thinking about anything too heavy.

And then it all ended.

The door to Hertz's Pizza opened. Debbie walked in. Normally, this would have been fine. She would have come over. Said hello. She might have eaten with them.

But not tonight.

Behind Debbie walked Mike Solomon. Chad knew Mike. He was a nice guy. He was on the track team.

He shouldn't be on a date with Debbie, though. Not yet. It's too soon.

Then Chad remembered hearing something about the two of them. He was always in such a fog at school. He probably didn't process it. Like his mind rejected the idea or something.

He kept staring at Debbie as a waiter led the couple to a booth.

"Are you okay?" Maria asked. She turned and saw what he was looking at. "Oh, Chad. Didn't you know about them?"

Chad looked at their food. Suddenly, just looking at their fresh meal was making him sick.

"Maybe." His tone was low.

"You wanna go?" Maria asked.

Chad looked into her eyes. All the happy was gone. She looked scared. He hated that he had taken away her happiness. But he couldn't help it.

Chapter 30

NOT IN THE MOOD

Maria was pressed against Chad in the driver's seat. Normally, it was reversed. Chad would go after her in the passenger seat. Or on a really good night, they would be in the back seat.

Tonight it was all wrong.

Before everything had happened, he would've loved having her go after him like that. Her lips and skin were so soft. Chad loved the way he would get tangled up in her long brown hair. She got him so excited all the time. He loved the game between them as she tried to calm him down.

Chad was kissing Maria. She was in his arms. He could feel her heart beating strongly against his chest. She seemed to be wrapping herself even tighter around him. Probably because she wasn't feeling anything from him.

"Are you okay?" Maria asked.

Chad looked at her. Her question bothered him.

"Yeah," he said.

He closed his eyes and started to kiss her again. He tried to put more into it. More feeling. More passion. Something to make things better with Maria. Like they had been before seeing Debbie and Mike.

"Don't worry about, Debbie."

"I won't," he said harshly.

Chad started to increase his grip on Maria. He pressed his face and mouth harder against her. He didn't know if it was because he wanted to show her that he was into what they were doing, or if he hoped she would stop talking.

His grip got tighter. And tighter.

"Hey!" Maria pushed Chad away from her. She sat back in her seat. "What's the matter? You were hurting me." Maria put her hand to her face.

"I'm sorry."

"Just be more gentle. Okay?" Maria started to move toward him.

Chad put up his hand and turned away from Maria. He turned on the ignition.

"Let's just go home," he said.

"Why?"

"I just wanna go home."

Before Maria could protest, Chad pulled the car into the street.

They didn't drive for more than five seconds before Maria put her hand on his. She squeezed his hand again. Chad tried to reciprocate but couldn't.

"Are you not into me anymore?"

Maria's voice was strained. "It's like you don't even want to be near me anymore."

"You were the one who stopped me." He eyed the road.

"I know you're upset about Debbie. I understand that, I guess."

Chad felt his anger surging. His best friend's girlfriend was with another guy. Marcus was barely in the ground and she was moving on.

"Do you not want to be homecoming king and queen?" Chad felt Maria looking at him. It was like she could see through him. But her questions were all wrong. "Are you just gonna be looking for reasons to be bummed out all the time? Chad—"

"Bummed out all the time?!" Chad shrieked. "My best friend died! I killed him! Nobody cares. Nobody wants to remember Marcus. Everyone thinks about it for just a little while. But you only want the sadness to be over!"

Chad was glaring at Maria. Her mouth was hanging open. She had never heard him sound so furious. His voice was beyond loud. It was filled with hurt and anger. Feelings she knew he had kept bottled up ever since Marcus died.

"It's never going to be over!" Chad continued. "Don't you think I want it to be? Don't you think I want everything to be okay? It isn't. It never will be again. I don't care about the things you care about anymore, Maria. I don't want to be homecoming king. It doesn't matter because we're all gonna die. You're gonna die. Everyone's gonna die!"

Chad was so upset. He didn't realize he had stopped in the middle of the street. There weren't many cars around, so nobody was honking.

Maria quickly undid her seatbelt and jumped out of the car.

Chapter 31

UNREAL EXPECTATIONS

It took some doing, but Chad eventually coaxed Maria back into the car. He apologized. But he didn't want to talk about his outburst. He couldn't bring himself to.

He meant what he had shouted. He wasn't happy about it. He was just glad he had revealed his thoughts. He was tired of being the only person who knew what he was thinking. He wasn't angry at Maria, but he wasn't *not* angry at her either.

When they got to her house, she bolted from his car before he could say anything.

It was just as well. He realized he still didn't have anything to say to her.

Before he knew it, he was parked across the street from Marcus's house. He wasn't directly across from it. Just close enough so he could see almost the entire front. He had been coming to this house his whole life. But now it felt foreign. Marcus's two-story house used to be so inviting. Now it looked as lifeless as Marcus was.

He stared at the red front door in the darkness. It had always been red. Chad couldn't help hoping that Marcus would walk out. Open that red door and appear.

Maybe he transferred schools.

Maybe he decided he wanted a different life.

A different best friend.

I don't care. At least he would be alive.

He closed his eyes. Chad told himself that when he opened them, it would be the first day of senior year again. They'd have fun driving to school just like before. They'd hang out with Maria and Debbie, go to Miss Scalf's class, and go out to lunch. This time, Chad would tell Marcus that they were going to cut practice and go to the beach. Just like Marcus had suggested.

The thought enveloped Chad. He couldn't help opening his eyes.

Nothing had changed.

The Pagel house was still dark and drab. The red door hadn't opened. Marcus hadn't come out of it.

And he wasn't going to.

Chapter 32

STUCK IN NEUTRAL

Come inside and get some rest," Chad's father said. "You're in training, remember?"

Chad was sitting in the car in the driveway. "Only the Young" was playing on repeat from his iPod. It had played about seven times before Chad's dad came out.

At first his dad asked what he was doing. He didn't answer. That was because he couldn't tell him. He'd been listening to his and Marcus's favorite song ever since he left Marcus's house. For Chad, there was no way to explain it. He *couldn't* turn the song off and get out of the car.

"You know I'm off the team," Chad said. "I have enough credits. Coach Mustain said I could just go home after fifth period. He said he'd work it out."

"I know. I was there, son." His dad's tone wasn't disappointed. He just sounded like he was trying to be empathetic.

A lone tear rolled down Chad's cheek. He didn't know why. He didn't feel sad. He didn't feel anything.

"You need to get help, Chad. You need to let out all those emotions. All that grief that's inside of you."

Chad nodded his head.

He didn't want to talk to his parents, Maria, or some stranger who was going to try and figure him out.

The only person I want to talk to is Marcus.

But Chad knew that was impossible.

Chapter 33

STAGES

Chad's dad eventually convinced him to come inside, and he went straight to his room.

He'd turned on his iPad, hoping to watch some videos. Instead, he Googled "grief." He clicked on a Wikipedia page that listed the five stages of grief.

Denial.

Anger.

Bargaining.

Depression.

Acceptance.

Chad sat there for a moment reading over the stages. The more he read what they were, the more his heart sank.

Chad had wanted to see them. His roadmap. Maybe he could pinpoint where he was and when all of this numbness would be over. It would give him something to look forward to.

All he saw were words.

He had no idea where he was within the stages. All he knew was that he felt lost.

2:00 p.m.

Chad was still lying in bed. He'd been staring at the ceiling for so long that he was starting to see patterns in the popcorn. Every time he thought about getting up, he realized that he didn't want to.

When he was training, he would have no problem dragging himself out and going for a run. Marcus always made it fun. Marcus often didn't want to run, so he'd crack jokes the entire time. This motivated Chad to train harder..

Chad's parents had looked in on him a few times.

"Do you need anything?" they asked. "You want some breakfast?"

Later they asked, "You up for some lunch?"

Chad either shook his head or gave his stock answer: "I'm not hungry."

Aside from lying in bed, he checked his phone. Maria hadn't called. After last night he hadn't really expected her to. Still, they usually spent Sundays together. But not since Marcus died. At least they'd talked. At least she'd tried.

I wonder if I wrecked it between us. I hope she calls.

He sure wanted her to. The only problem was that he had lost his ability to express anything.

And that really scared him.

When Marcus died, a part of Chad died too. The glass half-full part. The fun-loving part. He wondered if he was ever going to be the same.

Chapter 34

PANIC ATTACK

Realizing his parents were probably going to have an intervention if he continued staying in his room staring at the ceiling, he decided to go for a run. That had always made him feel good in the past. He hoped that once he got going, he'd get a runner's high.

That might snap me out of it.

Mile Square Park was a square mile of open green space, a lake, a golf course, and play areas. It was really close to his house. Families often spent their Sundays there. Chad and Marcus would weave in and out of kids on bikes, rollerbladers, and walkers when they ran the park's circuit.

Chad figured he'd start running. Hopefully he'd have enough endurance to go around a couple of times. There weren't that many people at the park that day. Thankfully.

After the first mile, Chad saw Marcus's family drive by. They were over a lane and hadn't seen him. Chad recognized their car the moment he saw it: a gray Honda Pilot. He also saw the silhouette of Dave's head in the backseat.

Chad had ridden with them a million times. He always sat in the backseat. Dave would sit in the middle. Marcus behind his mom. Chad behind Mr. Pagel. They never listened to music when they were all in the car. They never even turned the radio on. They just talked about everything.

Wrestling.

School.

Debbie.

Maria.

Girls Dave liked.

College.

Chad realized they probably weren't talking about any of that stuff now.

Suddenly he got a tight feeling in his chest. He figured it was a cramp. He had felt something similar before.

He kept running. But the tightness didn't go away.

"Keep going," he said out loud. He hoped he could power through this by sheer force of will.

The tightness continued. Then he felt the air leave his lungs. It was like nothing he'd ever experienced. His lungs deflated, like a balloon losing air.

He started walking. He put his hand on his chest. The tightness was still there. He could breathe but it was labored. He stopped walking and looked around.

Cars were driving by. In the distance people were walking and talking on their phones. Others were walking dogs or were with their kids.

He moved toward some people coming from the opposite direction. Then he stopped. Chad had no idea what was happening to him. But he didn't want to ask for help. He didn't want to bother anybody.

He sat down on a patch of grass. With his hand still on his chest, he looked up at the sky. There wasn't a cloud in sight.

Am I dying? Why is this happening? Calm down. I need to calm down. Take slow deep breaths.

He sat there. Scared. Alone. He thought he might die right then and there. Nobody was going to help him. And he didn't want them to.

Is this payback? I don't want to die.

He stayed on the grass for thirty minutes. Slowly, he found he was able to breathe easier. He could take in more air. And then the tightness in his chest went away. As if it had never been there.

AGAINST THE GRAIN

It was late Sunday evening. The pain and tightness hadn't come back. But that didn't mean Chad was feeling okay. Drinking beer made him feel better. And he figured drinking one now would relax him for the rest of the night.

He heard his parents leave. They were getting something to eat. They had asked him to go. As usual, he told them he just wanted to stay home. He always used to enjoy eating out with his parents. It was an Erickson family tradition to go out on Sunday evenings for as long as he could remember. But now he couldn't think of anything less he'd rather do. What would they talk about? What if he ran into friends from school?

Chad figured he was going to stay close to home for as long as he could. Maybe he'd do it until he started college. Unless he was able to go away for school. The only problem was he still needed wrestling to secure a scholarship.

He went to the kitchen and popped open one of his dad's beers. The moment he took a swig, he felt better. He was starting to enjoy how the beer felt as he drank it. The cold liquid. The tingle on his tongue. The bubbles at the back of his mouth. How it burned as it hit his stomach. The taste was just okay.

But it made him feel something. He liked that. He was so numb to every-thing now. As much as he was scared by what happened in the park, it had felt reassuring. It let Chad know he was still human. He could still feel.

He grabbed the first beer. Then he took another and headed to his room. As he walked down the hall, he made a mental note to slow down the drinking. His dad hardly ever drank beer. Maybe one per month. He wouldn't notice a beer or two missing. But if they were all gone, it would be a problem.

Then he remembered that his mom had bought some more last week. There was no space for them in the fridge, so she'd left them in the garage.

He put the unopened beer in his small fridge.

Chad lay down on his bed. He polished off what was left of the first beer. He was starting to drink them faster. Enjoy them too much.

Having that other beer in his fridge

made him sleep better than he had in a long time.

After breakfast the next morning, Chad went back to his room. He shut the door and opened up the beer he'd stored the night before. It burned his throat as he swallowed. The temperature in his mini-fridge was much colder than the one in the kitchen.

Again, he finished the beer off quickly. Then he brushed his teeth and headed to school.

Chapter 36

CLIMBING DOWNWARD

It was almost fifth period. Chad had been feeling pretty good all day. Things felt normal. He'd been talking to people. Getting his assignments done. And he'd only thought about Marcus a few times.

Normally, that would freak him out. He was afraid of forgetting Marcus. Like he thought everybody else had.

Today, though, he wasn't worried about it. He was just happy that he got through the day feeling okay.

The bell sounded.

Being kicked off the team still hurt.

No practice. No practical jokes. No sixth period. Every day he felt like a loser when he went home before his teammates.

He thought he had nothing. And the situation with Maria was making him feel even worse. They still hadn't talked since their date. Chad hadn't tried and they hadn't run into each other at school either.

Going home, he realized that he didn't feel too bad.

About anything.

He knew he had more than enough units to graduate. Only having four classes wasn't going to hurt him. Chad also knew that he and Maria would talk. Eventually.

On that sunny Monday afternoon, Chad didn't care about anything but feeling good again.

SICKNESS

A few days later Chad was walking home. It was not his day to use the car. Today his dad drove it.

As he walked, he passed Cliff's Liquor store. It was more than a store to buy booze. Cliff's sold candy. Soft drinks. Snacks. Deli sandwiches. Lottery tickets. He and Marcus had gone there since they were kids. It was under new ownership, but it still sold the same stuff.

Chad and Marcus always bought juices when they had to walk home. Marcus loved fruity drinks. Chad always liked cranberry juice. A lot of the students from Shepard High School went there at lunch.

Chad went in. He needed beer.

He felt weird being at Cliff's for alcohol. But he didn't have a choice. He wanted to drink more. His dad didn't drink enough to keep the supply coming. His parents would catch on soon enough. He had moved the new ones from the garage into the fridge. But he already drank three of those.

He discreetly went past the chips. He acted like he was looking for something. Cliff's had many middle school kids inside looking for snacks.

They must have a minimum day or something. They're like a mini-swarm. Jeez.

Good for him. The person behind the counter seemed more concerned with watching the kids than he did with watching Chad.

He took his backpack and slowly unzipped it. He grabbed a six-pack of the same brand he'd been drinking. He turned down a candy aisle. As Chad looked at the candy, he gently set the six-pack inside his backpack. He continued walking and slowly zipped up his bag.

He had done it. There was no turning back now.

Chad stopped and looked at some candy bars. Leaving too fast would arouse suspicion. He and Marcus were not as friendly with the new owner as they had been with Cliff.

Chad walked to the door. He tried to remain calm. *Breathe. You didn't do anything wrong. You need this beer. You're just taking care of yourself.*

"No way! Those are gross," a familiar voice said.

It was Dave. Marcus's brother.

Chad didn't look back. He figured

Dave and a friend were looking at chips or something. The boy hadn't seen Chad.

Chad knew if he kept walking, then Dave wouldn't see him.

Seeing and talking to Dave would be worse than getting caught. If he spoke to Dave, he'd have to talk about Marcus.

He'd have to acknowledge that his friend was dead.

He'd have to acknowledge what had happened. What he had done.

The bells on the door chimed as Chad walked out. He left without being seen. His shoplifting unnoticed. When he got far enough away, he started to run.

He didn't stop until he was home.

Chapter 38

BAD MEMORIES

A beer bottle made clanking sounds as it hit against some others. Chad had thrown it across the room into the wastepaper basket. He made a mental note to remove the evidence from his room. He'd been sneaking out the empty bottles and dropping them into the recycle bin.

As Chad lay back on his bed, he felt himself grinning. He felt great. He'd drunk two of the beers he'd stolen. He was buzzed. He tried to hide the remaining four bottles behind some blue ice packs in his bedroom fridge.

Aside from some work on his English project, Chad had gotten all of his homework done at school. He laughed a little when he realized that the English project was still on the *The Hangover*.

Chad wished he'd felt as good earlier as he did now. He could've talked to Dave in the liquor store. When he was filled with liquid courage, he could talk to anybody.

He turned on the TV. *Step Brothers* was on. It was one of Marcus's favorite movies. His too. Chad started laughing. He stretched himself out on his bed and got comfortable.

But his happiness slowly started to drain away. It was gone as quickly as it had come. He started thinking about Marcus. About all their plans for senior year. About the lifetime of fun they'd had. From trading lunches in elementary school. To going gaga for girls in middle school. To planning for college in high school. It all came back.

Chad was transported to the wrestling room. He was watching him and Marcus wrestle. It was the final moment of their match. Chad slammed Marcus to the mat.

"No!" he said out loud.

And just like that, he was back in his room.

Step Brothers was still on. But it was no longer making him laugh. Chad looked around his room and realized he had never felt this low.

Even if the alcohol-induced happiness wasn't real, he wanted it back. He wanted another beer. He wanted to escape.

So he did.

Chapter 39

STARING INTO THE SUN

Chad's eyes were closed as he sat on a bench waiting for the first period bell to sound. For the past few weeks, he had been trying to arrive at school the split second before his second period English class started. Today he had shown up early.

He drank too much the night before and felt sick. He'd thought about staying home. But he didn't want to worry his parents. They'd come in and start snooping around, maybe find the beers.

The morning sun washed over him. It made him feel worse. With the bright light and heat, Chad felt like he was under a spotlight. He was burning up. He wanted to move but he felt queasy. He'd only sat on the bench to steady his stomach. Now he felt like he couldn't move. He sure hoped this would go away. And soon.

"Hey." Maria was sitting next to him now. Chad didn't even notice her walk up to him.

"Hi." He opened his eyes, realizing he probably looked strange to her.

"How have you been?" Her voice was saying one thing, but Chad knew she was thinking another.

"Good." He took a deep a breath. He wanted to see if breathing air was going to make him feel sicker. It didn't.

"Are you okay?" Chad avoided Maria's gaze. The last thing he wanted was to have a serious conversation.

"Yeah, I'm great." He tried to smile. He couldn't.

I should think of something funny to say. But I feel like crap.

"I've been thinking," Maria started. "You need some time alone, Chad. You don't seem like you want to be around people anymore. You need to talk to somebody about what you're going through. How you're acting … your anger. It's not good for you."

Chad nodded his head. He wanted to say more. He wanted to fight for Maria. He wanted to be the person he had been before Marcus died.

He couldn't. Not right now anyway.

"I'll talk to you later." Maria was gone before Chad had even realized she'd left.

God, I suck. I need to go after her. I need to tell her how much I want to go to the homecoming dance with her. I'll tell her we just need to be together.

But the sun was too bright. Maria was lost in the crowd of students.

Chapter 40

THE HANGOVER

Chad knew that the presentation for *The Hangover* was coming up. But he didn't realize it was that day. The group had worked on it some, but he didn't participate.

"We're … we're next," Eliza stammered. "Do you know what you're going to say? Chad! What are you going to say?"

She was staring hard at Chad. It was like she could see through him. She knew he wasn't ready. He figured she was probably glad. She had never liked him or Marcus much. She was a serious student.

She just saw them as jocks. Any sympathy she'd had for him after Marcus died was gone. Like everybody else, she wanted him to get over it.

"He'll be fine," Noah Jackson said. He put his arm around Chad for emphasis. The team had originally been Chad, Marcus, Joe, and Eliza. Noah took Marcus's spot. He was a heavyweight on the wrestling team.

"Yeah, Chad's got this." Joe held up his hand. Chad high-fived him. He smiled too.

Chad had no idea what he was going to say. He was just hoping he could do it. He told himself to do it for Marcus. That only gave him slightly more confidence.

Eliza, Joe, and Noah talked about why *The Hangover* was a good movie. They made good arguments. Chad was surprised that Eliza actually made an argument for the movie. She had fought Marcus when he suggested the topic.

Now it was Chad's turn. He slowly walked to the front of the class with some quick notes. Joe and Noah had helped him.

All I have to do is read the notes. Just read. Then I can sit down.

But there was a problem. As he glanced at his notes, he realized he couldn't read his scribbles.

Everyone stared at him, waiting. Miss Scalf watched from the back of the classroom. She had her grade book in front of her. She seemed to sense something wasn't right. But she wasn't saying anything. Many people wanted Chad to move on. To get over it. But people like Miss Scalf, Maria, his parents, they would always be there for him. Even if he kept pushing them away.

Then Chad saw Marcus's desk. A guy Chad didn't know was sitting there. He stared at Chad. He must have known what happened to Marcus, but he didn't really care about it. He was just sitting in the desk Miss Scalf assigned. Chad couldn't believe he hadn't noticed before now.

Chad couldn't take his eyes off the desk. He knew he had to. He knew he had to say something.

He opened his mouth. That's when he threw up.

He dropped to one knee as he caught his breath.

He never took his eyes off of Marcus's old desk.

Chapter 41

WALKING DEAD

Chad felt a lot better after he vomited. He wanted to stay in school. But he couldn't. The rule at Shepard High was that if you threw up, you had to go home.

So now Chad found himself walking home mid-morning. The office staff offered to call his parents since his dad had the car. But he lived close enough to the school that they told him he could walk.

He started thinking about how good it would feel to lie down on his bed. Drink some more beers. Get lost in the haze.

That's when he realized that he only

had one left. He knew he shouldn't have drank so many last night. But he couldn't help it. They made him feel good. They helped him forget. His problems disappeared when he drank.

He could drink the beers in the big fridge. But his parents would notice they were gone. And with Chad being home, it wouldn't be too hard for them to figure out who had taken them.

He walked by Cliff's again. Before he knew it, he heard the store's door jingle as he went inside.

He slowly unzipped his backpack notch by notch. He pretended like he was looking at something else in the cooler aisle. Then he slipped a six-pack inside his bag.

He overheard the man behind the counter talking with some customers.

Does he recognize me from the other day? Does he count the six-packs and know one was missing? Chad thought. *Stop! I'm just being paranoid. Just play it cool.*

Out of the corner of his eye, he noticed small bottles of whiskey. It was a label he recognized. He thought it was a cool drink. Something that real men drank.

He and Marcus had sipped some once at a family party. They both spit it out. But how would it taste now? He was curious.

Chad put the small bottle in his backpack too. He slid it in very gently so that it wouldn't make a noise against the other bottles already there.

Chad looked around again, pretending to examine some chips.

He was going to have a great day as soon as he got home.

The bells jingled as Chad walked out of Cliff's.

Before the door closed, the clerk and another man grabbed him. The clerk was skinny except for a potbelly. The other man was short and muscular. Chad had never seen him in Cliff's before.

"What's in the backpack?" the clerk asked.

"Nothing," Chad said.

"Come on." The shorter guy put his hand on the zipper of the backpack. Then he hesitated.

Chad figured that legally, he couldn't open the bag.

"We saw you," the clerk said. "Shouldn't you be in school?"

Chad wished he was. He just stared silently at the clerk.

"Make it easy on yourself. Open your bag," the short man said.

"The police are already on their way. Either they open your bag, or you do it."

Chad took a deep breath. He put his hands on his backpack.

He knew he should be afraid. He knew

he should try to run. He knew these guys probably couldn't make him open his backpack.

But he opened it anyway. Despite knowing he was in a world of trouble, he felt a weird sense of relief.

"Let's go back inside," the clerk said as he took the beer and whiskey out of Chad's backpack.

Chapter 42

CONTINUING THE CLIMB DOWNWARD

The police asked the store clerk a few questions. Then the officer tried to talk to Chad. But Chad wasn't responding. The officer asked to see his ID. Chad said nothing. The officer then frisked him but didn't find an ID.

The officer continued to question him. Chad stayed silent. He didn't know why he was acting like this. Every time he told himself to talk, nothing came out.

After reading Chad his rights, the officer cuffed him. The handcuffs were tight but not so tight that Chad felt like they were hurting his skin. Then the officer gently escorted Chad to the squad car and put him in. Chad expected them to turn on the lights and the siren as the officer took him to the station.

There was none of that.

As Chad waited in the squad car, he saw some students from Shepard High driving by. Chad had no idea how long he had been in Cliff's. But he figured since students were going to lunch, he'd been detained for a while.

He expected to feel nervous. To feel something. But he didn't feel anything. And that was scary.

The police officer talked a bit on his radio, but it was in code. Chad didn't know what all the numbers meant. The officer didn't try to talk to Chad again. He didn't lecture him. He didn't ask why he did it. He didn't even ask why Chad wasn't in school.

Chad was taken to the police station. It didn't go down like he'd seen in the movies. He thought processing would take a long time.

It didn't.

He was told where to stand to get his picture taken. Then he was taken to a desk where his backpack was. He was asked to empty his pockets of personal items. The only thing Chad had were his house keys.

After that he was fingerprinted. Chad wasn't asked a single question. He still hadn't spoken. He figured the officers would get his information eventually, and they would call his parents.

Once he had been "rolled" as the person taking his prints said, Chad was taken down to a small holding cell. Nobody else was there. It had a bed and nothing else.

At first, Chad was afraid to sit on the bed, so he stood. Then he sat on the floor.

I wish I had a beer. Or at least my iPod. How did I get here? God, I am in so much trouble. And it's my fault.

But he still felt numb. After getting arrested. After getting kicked off the wrestling team. After getting dumped by Maria. After being distant with his parents. He felt absolutely nothing.

He started to feel sad after thinking about Marcus. It was the same kind of grief he felt when watching *Step Brothers*.

Chad tried to think of something else—anything else—but he couldn't. He kept seeing Marcus's face. Marcus was staring at him. He didn't smile. His expression was serious. Then he started to shake his head.

Wherever Marcus is, he's disappointed in me, Chad thought.

Forget senior year, this wasn't how Chad was supposed act. Marcus knew it and Chad did too.

Chapter 43

AGAINST THE WORLD

The sun was almost down as Chad rode home from the police station with his parents.

As they pulled into their neighborhood, he noticed some kids playing kickball. Other kids were hanging around on the sidewalk talking and texting. He saw a few taking selfies.

"I just don't understand why you didn't say anything," his dad said for what seemed like the fiftieth time. "The arresting officer said he would have had us come to the liquor store. He didn't want to take you down to the station. We could've taken you home. Now this whole mess is bigger than it needs to be."

Chad hadn't said anything to his parents yet. He wasn't trying to be rude. He just didn't have any idea what to say.

What does everybody want from me? What do I want from me? I'm so confused.

"You need help." His mom had turned around in her seat and was looking at him now. "It's not on your terms anymore, Chad. You have to see a judge." She choked back tears as she spoke. "I just don't know why you're doing this. We all miss Marcus. But this is no way to act."

"Your mother's right, Chad."

Chad wasn't looking at his dad, but he could feel his eyes on him from the rearview mirror.

"You're not going to like it, but you're going to have to do it. You *need* to do it. Not just for the people who want you to get help. You have to do it for yourself," his dad said.

All these words. It was like throwing water against a wall. They were just trickling down. The words weren't sinking in. They weren't making any impact. Soon, they'd dry up and go away.

For the kids outside, today was a normal day. Nothing was different than yesterday.

Chad wanted that again, but he knew he was too far gone.

Chapter 44

HEART TO HEART

Chad lay on his bed not doing anything. He had been like that for almost an hour. His mom had gone out to buy a pizza.

There was a knock at his door.

"Chad?" his father asked cautiously.

Chad stared at the door. He wanted to be alone, but he knew he had to say something.

"Y-yeah?" he kind of croaked. His voice sounded weird. He figured it was probably because he hadn't spoken for many hours.

The door to his bedroom opened. His dad slowly walked in. He took a chair that was facing Chad's computer and turned it around so that now it was facing the bed.

"You know we love you, Chad."

They made eye contact. Chad nodded his head. As he did, he noticed that his father had tears in his eyes. "Your mother and I, we're blaming ourselves. We haven't been there for you enough. But you pushed us away. We thought you were dealing. We should've tried harder ..."

His dad caught himself. He took a deep breath, the way that people do when they're trying to stifle a sob.

"I'm scared for you, Chad. Your mother and I are terrified about what's happening. You're going to go before a judge in open court. I tried like hell to have the hearing in chambers. But you weren't saying anything. I think he may want to make an example out of you. He probably thinks you're some punk kid. But you're not. We all know you're not."

Tears were flowing down his father's cheeks. He wasn't making any effort to stop them.

"Your mom and I, we can only help you so much. You have to want this. You have to want to get better. You've been spending so much time in this room." His Dad looked around. It was like he hadn't really seen it since Chad was a little kid. "I've never had to worry about you before. I'm not good at it. I wish I was a better father to you right now."

His dad was getting even more choked up. They stared at each other for a little while longer. Then his dad got up and left the room.

God. I feel like that chat was more for him than for me. He eyed the fridge. *The beer is all gone. What am I going to do?*

He got up and went over to his closet. Between piles of clothes, some old wrestling trophies, and other boxes, he took out a photo album.

Chad opened it. There was a photo of him and Marcus right in front. It was from their first day of kindergarten. They were standing together by the swings. Chad's head was a mop of brownish blond hair. Marcus's black hair sported a bowl cut.

Chad slowly stared at the picture. He realized he was having trouble breathing again. The air felt like it was leaving his lungs. It was just like before. Like the day in the park. Maybe worse.

Chad was frozen. He couldn't look away from the photograph.

Chapter 45

STANDING SMALL BEFORE THE MAN

Chad didn't know what he was expecting from the open court session with Judge De La Garza, but this wasn't it.

He was standing at the defendant's table with a public defender, who he hadn't met until that morning. Even Chad's parents didn't know he was going to be there. Across from them was a prosecutor. Near the public defender were five inmates wearing orange jumpsuits.

Chad didn't know why the judge was

making him go through this. He wasn't like the guys in the orange jumpsuits. Earlier, he had been sitting with his parents and the public defender in the back of the courtroom. He watched the judge lecture a few inmates who were no longer in the courtroom.

Every time an inmate would stand before the judge, the prosecutor, the public defender, and the judge would talk while the inmate stood. Chad thought the inmates were passive.

Why don't they say anything? Why don't they stand up for themselves?

His best friend was dead. He was going through a tough time. He had made a mistake trying to steal alcohol. He knew he just needed time. He would be okay.

"The defendant knows he's going to have to attend mandatory grief counseling." Judge De La Garza looked up from her paperwork as she eyed Chad.

"Yes, Your Honor," the public defender said.

This made Chad angry. He never liked having people decide things for him. He really hated it now.

He eyed his parents, who were sitting behind him on long benches. Chad could tell by their expressions that they agreed with the judge. They had wanted him to get counseling, but he hadn't listened. Now he had no choice.

"Chad," Judge De La Garza said, getting his attention. "I know you've been through a tough time losing your friend, but you've got to face this."

Chad wanted to scream. He hadn't just lost a friend. Marcus was his *best* friend. Chad hated hearing the judge talk like she could understand anything about him. She didn't know him or Marcus.

"You're also very lucky that you have parents who care enough about you to see that you get help. Since this is only your first offense, I'm accepting a misdemeanor plea. In addition to grief counseling, you're also going to have to a attend a session of petty larceny counseling."

Chad felt all the muscles in his face tighten.

"Chad, when you're grieving, isolation is your enemy," the judge continued. "Many times, the sad and confused want to be alone. They close themselves off from family and friends—the people who care about them the most. You will not be that person on my watch. You will follow through with this. You will live up to your responsibilities. Then this case will be dismissed. You can move on to bigger and better things. If you don't? I may just see you over there."

The judge motioned to the inmates. Chad didn't look at them. He didn't have to. He could feel their eyes on him.

Chapter 46

FREAK SHOW

A few days later Chad came home from school, finished his homework, and went for a walk. The grief counseling wasn't set up yet.

He wanted to stay in his room, but he was worried that his parents would freak out. Ever since the judge made it clear that he had to get help, he felt as if his parents were acting differently toward him. Watching his every move. The trust was gone.

Chad walked for a long time. He didn't

know where he was going. He put on his running clothes, but he didn't feel like running. Eventually, he found himself walking past the cemetery where Marcus was buried. He didn't know why, but he decided to go in.

As he walked, he saw noticed there were only a few people visiting. They were mostly older people. They stood across from tombstones and talked to them, like they were talking to the actual person. Some put out flowers or cleaned up old ones that had died or fallen over.

In the distance, Chad saw the location where Marcus was buried. There was no headstone yet, but he knew it was Marcus's spot.

For a moment, he thought about going over to the grave.

I sure could use a good talk with Marcus right now. My life is so messed up.

But he whipped around and walked out of the cemetery. He didn't want to go there mentally. But he felt he had to do it. Eventually. He tried to convince himself that Marcus wasn't really *there-there* anyway. It was just his body, not his soul.

Chapter 47

GRIEF GROUP

He was everything to me. But we didn't always get along. He could be really stubborn. I miss him so much." Angelique sobbed as she spoke with Chad and June. Angelique was talking about her father. He had died of cancer a month ago.

June was the moderator of Chad's grief support group. Chad and Angelique were the only people there. The room had cream-colored wallpaper and soothing pictures of the sky and ocean on the wall. Chairs were set up in a semi-circle.

"I just …" she continued as she choked

back tears. "All I think about when I see him in my mind is how much he suffered."

Chad looked at the tan carpet on the floor. He thought about Marcus. Then he started to get mad.

At least she had had some time with her father before he died. At least she had gotten the chance to say goodbye. She had the benefit of knowing she was going to lose him.

Chad looked up at Angelique. She had long black hair and olive-colored skin. She was wearing a T-shirt and jeans. Chuck Taylors. For a brief moment, Chad thought she could be really pretty if she used a little makeup.

Angelique continued talking. Chad figured she was older than him but not by much.

Eventually, the group session ended. Neither June nor Angelique made mention of the fact that Chad hadn't said a word.

He figured they were going easy on him because it was his first day.

As he walked out of the building, he saw Angelique getting into her car across the parking lot. She waved at him and he waved back.

Chad didn't know how old Angelique was. What he did know was that she was a lot better at dealing with grief than he was.

Chapter 48

SPORTS DAY

There was an event taking place in the main plaza of Shepard High. The plaza was surrounded by lunch tables and places students could buy food.

Sports Day was primarily for school athletes. Kids from different sports competed against one another in various fun events. The school had sports days every few months. They were designed to promote unity and good sportsmanship among the athletes and the entire student body.

Chad was walking out of the school

when he saw what was happening. He had competed in Sports Day every year since he was a freshman. Because he wasn't on the wrestling team, he didn't even know it was scheduled until he saw it.

He watched for a moment as Ryan Abad and Tighe Nishamura tried to play some guys on the basketball team in a hoops contest. Ryan and Tighe were mainly throwing up air balls. Everybody was laughing and having a good time.

For a brief moment, he thought about going over and watching his friends.

Then he saw Debbie and Mike organizing another event. He didn't know what event they were doing, but he figured it had something to do with tennis because they both had racquets.

Instantly, Chad lost all interest.

As he turned to leave, his eyes made contact with Maria's. She was standing on a planter with some friends. They were watching the competition.

She smiled at Chad and waved. He smiled slightly. He stared into her green eyes for as long as he could.

Chapter 49

SELF-EDGE

Chad tried not to walk too quickly. Every time he moved, he heard the beers he'd stolen clink around in his backpack. He didn't want to steal anymore, but he couldn't help it.

Seeing Maria. Seeing Debbie with a guy who wasn't Marcus. Not being a part of the events at school. It was all too much. After he left school, he went to the supermarket's alcohol section. He took a cold six-pack of beer and put it in his backpack.

Once he was out of the store, he felt like he could breathe again. He made it.

Chad had stolen more beers and didn't get caught. He was going to feel okay for as long as the alcohol lasted.

"Chad!" he heard a voice call.

At first he thought he'd been caught. But nobody coming after him for stealing would know his name.

It was worse.

Chad turned around and saw Dave. He was across the street with some friends. They were riding home from school. They were all wearing backpacks

Chad froze. He didn't know what to do. He certainly couldn't hide.

Dave waved at him.

Chad managed to bring up his hand and wave back slightly. Then he started walking away. He thought about running but he didn't.

He started breathing fast.

Chad Erickson couldn't believe how scared he was of Marcus's family now.

His second family was gone. Just like Marcus.

He felt tears roll down his face. He wiped them away and clenched his back-pack. He was happy he'd stolen the beers.

They were all he had.

Chapter 50

SPILLING GUTS

The light outside was fading into the evening sky as Chad started his second beer. He had taken his small fridge and put it in his closet. There was an outlet there. He put some clothes on it. Nobody could see unless they really looked. He was putting the empty bottles into a paper bag under his bed. He planned take them to the trash.

He was looking through the old photo album that was filled with pictures of him and Marcus. He was transfixed on a picture from when they were in middle school. For a week in PE, their school had introduced wrestling. That was when Chad and Marcus got into the sport. They wrestled against other kids and learned the moves.

The picture showed them messing around. Chad had Marcus in a headlock. Marcus was grabbing Chad's lower body.

Then Chad remembered how he had grabbed Marcus the same way. How he slammed him to the mat. Marcus never got up. Chad could still picture him lying on that mat. Not moving.

Why did I kill you?

He spilled some of his beer on the photo album.

A cold jolt went through his body. He grabbed a dirty shirt off the bed and started mopping up the beer. He was furious at himself. These pictures—his memories—were all he had left of his best friend.

He had almost ruined one of them.

He was so angry with himself that he walked over to his bathroom sink and poured the rest of the beer down the drain.

He then made sure the photo album was okay. He looked through the entire book and was relieved to see that the beer hadn't done any true damage.

Chapter 51

ANGER

Chad sat in the support group. Other than him, June and Angelique were the only people there again.

Angelique had been talking about her dad. From everything she said, Chad thought he sounded like a cool guy. He had been in the U.S. Air Force. He wrote poetry. He was always there for his family. No matter what.

Now there was a lull in the conversation. Chad hated the quiet because he knew somebody else was supposed to share.

June and Angelique wanted to hear from Chad.

"What do you want me to say?" he asked after a long pause.

"Anything you want," Angelique replied.

June nodded her head.

Chad didn't look at them. He didn't want to talk. But he knew he had to. It was part of his court-mandated treatment. Chad knew the court was going to keep tabs on his progress.

He briefly thought about how great it would be to be back in his bedroom.

But sitting alone and drinking in his room wasn't helping so much anymore. And Chad knew it.

"Well," he started. "I want my friend Marcus back so we can have our senior year together."

"You feel that's been taken from you,"

June said as a statement of fact. That made Chad feel good.

"Yeah." His voice cracked.

He started to feel himself getting emotional. He could feel tears forming. It was already hard to speak.

"I feel the same way about my father. I feel what you're going through," Angelique offered.

Chad stared at her. He looked at June.

He was nervous.

Chad started to wonder if maybe the real reason he didn't talk to people about Marcus was not because he didn't think people cared. Maybe it was because if he did, he might begin healing from his loss. He might get over it.

And if he did heal, then all he would have left of Marcus might disappear.

"So." June smiled warmly. "Tell us about your friend. Tell us whatever you want to about him."

Chad felt tears slowly come down his nose.

"Well," his tone was low as he started. "Marcus was a great guy."

Chapter 52

COFFEE

I work at a bar," Angelique stated as she and Chad waited for the elevator.

The grief support meeting was over.

"Oh."

"I've seen the way you look at me. Like, 'Why's this old lady in my group?' " She smiled after she said that. It was only then that Chad noticed a small tattoo on one of her arms. It spelled the name Logan. Chad wondered if that was her husband, or maybe her boyfriend. Then he remembered she mentioned having a son named Logan.

He was five. She said he was helping her cope with the loss of her father.

It seemed weird when Chad first heard that. That a little kid could help an adult with their problems.

"I wasn't able to come to the meetings at night," Angelique continued.

Chad was a person of few words. This made other people talk more. "So, since I'm only twenty-two and you're the only person here, they let me come to the teen group."

Chad nodded his head. He felt like an idiot not saying more, but he honestly had no idea what to say to her.

"I like what you said about your friend." She smiled at him.

"I don't feel that much better," Chad offered. He had a hard time with normal conversations, but he had no problem being negative now.

"You will. This whole thing, it's a process."

The bell for the elevator dinged and the doors opened. Chad followed Angelique into it.

"I was a basket case before I started talking to June. It was just her and me for the first couple of months."

"Uh-huh."

Angelique looked at her phone.

"I have an hour before my shift starts. You want to get some coffee?" She smiled at him again.

Chad liked her smile. Not because he was interested in her or anything. He was still in love with Maria. He just liked being smiled at. It was a lot better than having everybody walking on eggshells around him. Staring at him. Talking behind his back. Whispering.

DENIAL

I just don't see the point in all that now."
Chad was trying to keep his voice low.

He and Angelique had gone to a
nearby coffee shop. They were sitting outside. She was drinking coffee. Chad didn't
like coffee, so he got an iced tea.

"We're all gonna die anyway," he said.

Chad told Angelique everything.
Unlike in the group, he did most of the
talking, to his surprise.

"You realize everybody goes through
this. You know?" Her eyes were fixed on
him. "When they lose somebody."

"Yeah, this stuff happens. I want to move on. But nobody's letting me. They're making me go to that stupid group—"

"That group is not stupid," Angelique said sharply. "That group is how I've been able to exist since my father died."

Her eyes didn't waver. Angelique was holding Chad's eyes in her gaze. She wasn't going to let him off the hook.

"You better wise up, kid."

"I'm not a kid."

"Stop." She held up her index finger and continued staring at him. "You lost somebody. Your best friend. I lost my dad. He was my best friend. That doesn't mean you get to trash your life. Shut everybody else out. You only get to be a senior once. You better start enjoying it."

"How? I hate everything now." Chad was starting to get mad.

"You're going to college. Yes?"

"Yeah. So what?"

"You're gonna be starting all over. Nobody is gonna think you're special anymore. Nobody's gonna care that you lost your best friend."

"Nobody cares now."

"You care."

Chad's bottom lip quivered. He knew Angelique saw it. He didn't care.

"I'm not trying to be mean," she went on. "I just want you to realize that life goes on. Even after your best friend dies."

"But …" Chad's voice cracked. "I lost my best friend. I killed him."

"You didn't kill him. It was an accident. Look, I know it hurts." She put her hand on his. Her skin was coarser than Maria's. "It's sad. It's tragic. And there's no real explanation. Nothing anybody is gonna say or do is gonna make it better. The only thing you can do is honor him. Mourn. And not ruin your life. You think Marcus would want you to do that?"

Chapter 54

LAZY SATURDAY

Normally, Chad did his homework on Sunday afternoon. It was an old habit.

By Saturday morning he'd gotten all of his schoolwork done. He thought he would have two days to hide in his room and drink the four remaining beers. He knew he wanted more, but he wasn't going to worry about it just now.

He checked Reddit, YouTube, MovieWeb, TVweb, and other websites he liked. He watched the news and newly posted videos. Saturdays were always a snooze online unless something major happened.

He turned on the TV, sipping a beer as he flipped channels. There was nothing on that he wanted to watch. He swallowed some more of the beer. It didn't taste very good. It was warm.

He got up to put it in the fridge. As he did, he passed the window. His dad was working in the yard. Chad had heard him complaining about how one of the sprinkler heads was broken.

Chad was always impressed by how hard both of his parents worked. Their home was modest. But his parents worked hard to make it as nice as they could. His dad worked full-time and his mom worked part-time. They never complained about money, even though Chad knew they didn't have a lot.

Chad didn't work to contribute

financially. He felt he did his part by being a good student and working hard in school.

Instead of walking to the mini-fridge in his closet, he walked into his bathroom. He poured the warm beer down the drain. Tossed the empty bottle. And walked out of his room.

Chapter 55

A SIMPLE GESTURE

Hey," Chad said.

His dad looked up. He squinted at Chad from under his gardener's hat.

"Hi." His dad seemed startled. He wasn't used to seeing his son outside.

"You need help with that sprinkler head?" Chad indicated the tool his dad was using.

"I think I almost got it."

"Oh," Chad replied

"I still have some weeds to pull. I also want to sprinkle some fertilizer on the grass." Chad's father pointed to some tools and bags that he'd brought out from the garage.

"I'll get started on the weeds." Chad walked over and picked up a forked tool with a long metal shaft. He had been helping his dad with the yard since he was a little kid.

"We should get some ice cream after this. You used to love that."

"Dad, you are reading my mind. That sounds great."

Lately, Chad only thought about the past. Things seemed so much better then. Safer.

"I'll never get back on the wrestling team eating ice cream." Chad got on his knees and sank the weed-pulling tool into the ground. He knew he was going to get hot in the sun. But it felt good to be outside.

"You'll get back on the team," his dad reassured him.

Chapter 56

BARGAINING

Chad was running. Before he knew it, he passed Dave Pagel with a friend. They were both riding kick scooters.

If Chad had been paying attention, he would've avoided Dave. But he was just running in the park. Cars were zooming past him on the nearby street. Chad turned a corner as Dave came around it.

They made eye contact.

Dave stopped. His friend stopped.

So did Chad.

"Where have you been?" Dave asked. It was like nothing had happened. No time had passed. "When are you gonna come over?"

Chad felt his hand shaking. It wasn't that bad, though.

"Soon. I've been busy."

"How's wrestling? We wanna come see you. My parents. Me."

Marcus's parents want to see me wrestle. They probably want to see me lose. Chad thought. *Calm down. Calm down. Breathe.*

"You should come over. I'm lifting weights now. Maybe you could show me a few things. I liked it when you and Marcus used to lift in the garage."

Dave was smiling at Chad. He wanted to be friends. He wasn't mad. His parents probably weren't either.

Chad didn't know that for sure, though.

"I will." Chad wanted to believe he would not flake.

"When?"

Dave was still smiling. Still happy to be talking with Chad in spite of what had happened.

Chad knew they were going to have to talk about Marcus's death sometime.

Should I bring it up now? Should I say I am sorry about what happened to Marcus?

Dave's phone rang. He took it out of his pocket and glanced at it.

"Is it Cassie?" Dave's friend asked.

"I think so. I haven't saved her number yet."

Chad saw his moment to exit.

"Hey," he started to jog off. "You have my number. Call me."

"Okay."

"Talk to that girl now. It's more important. We'll catch up later."

Dave stared at him oddly for a moment. Then he smiled.

"Later, Chad," he said.

"Later, dude," Chad called back.

Chad continued on his run. He heard Dave laugh as he answered the phone.

Dave could use me around, Chad thought. *I'm not his big brother, but I could still help him out.*

Chapter 57

SHOCK THE MONKEY

The buzz of the convenience store door got Chad's attention. He saw two kids—they couldn't have been older than twelve—walk in. They went to the soft drink section. He figured they would check out the candy next. Just like when he and Marcus were kids.

And they did.

Chad eyed the beers in the cooler section. He didn't have his backpack with him. He could only steal one. He was looking for the biggest bottle he could hide in his running shirt.

He felt good after chatting with Dave. But the meeting had stressed him out. It had been intense for him. And he'd even cried a little.

"Stop it, jerk!" one of the kids said to his friend. They started messing around, punching and pushing each other. It was friendly play, not mean. It was the way Chad and Marcus goofed off.

If somebody got hurt, it was always an accident.

Always.

In that moment, Chad realized that so many things reminded him of Marcus.

And that wasn't bad.

This is what it means to have memories. This is what it means to care about somebody.

Chad had been trying to cope with Marcus's death by hiding from the world. But that just gave him more time to replay the accident. So he turned to alcohol, which made things worse.

Talking to Dave had been hard, but it also made him feel better. He figured the more he reconciled his past, the better he would feel. This meant confronting his fears about Marcus's death.

Chad had wanted to keep his spot on the wrestling team. He didn't hurt Marcus on purpose. He would never do that. He'd never forget Marcus.

"You boys stop it. Buy what you're gonna buy or get out!" the clerk yelled at the two kids.

Chad smiled as he left the convenience store empty-handed. He and Marcus used to annoy store clerks and get yelled at like that too.

Chapter 58

COMEBACK

Coach Mustain eyed Chad as he walked into the coaching office. He shared the space with three other coaches. Each had their own work area. The wall near Coach Mustain was lined with pictures of every wrestling team he'd trained.

Coach's area was large enough for a desk, a computer, a bookshelf, some family photos, and two chairs facing the desk. There was also a photo of a much younger Coach Mustain. He was in his wrestling uniform. Next to him was a man Chad had always assumed was Coach's father. The engraved frame read: A great father always. RIP.

Chad had seen this picture many times, but the engraving had never hit him the way it did now.

Everybody loses somebody. Everybody dies. I realize that now. This is why I have to live in the present.

"Hey, stranger." Coach Mustain smiled at Chad.

"Hi, Coach."

"How are you doing?" Coach tilted his head and waited for Chad to answer.

"Good. I'm doing a lot better." Chad looked at the ground. He was getting nervous. He tried to focus on his breathing. The last thing he wanted to do was freak out in front of this man. He'd never let him wrestle again. "I'm talking to somebody now."

"That's good. I told you that you needed to do that. It's healthy when you go through something so painful." Coach Mustain leaned back in his chair.

"I'm still really sad about everything that happened. But I'm dealing with it. I think."

"Just take it day by day."

"Yeah."

Chad figured he would never wrestle for the school again. He was done. The way Coach was talking to him, he probably figured Chad was a basket case. That he'd never get over Marcus.

"I think I'm dealing with it the right way now," Chad went on.

"I'll bet you are."

"It's not easy," Chad said.

"So," Coach Mustain stared Chad right in the eyes. "You think you're ready to come back? We sure could use you."

After Marcus died, nobody wanted to wrestle at one seventy. Jeff Coyle had come down from one eighty-two. He only did it because he thought he might be stronger. Instead, he was weaker. He lost every match.

"Yeah, I'm ready to come back," Chad said confidently. "For real this time."

Chapter 59

ANOTHER REALITY CHECK

On Saturday morning Chad reported to the courthouse for petty larceny counseling. A police detective lectured for six hours. Students followed along in a packet and filled in the blanks on their worksheets as she spoke. There were three twenty-minute breaks. Before each break, you had to turn in your completed worksheets.

Completing the worksheets was not optional. If you didn't finish, you had to catch up. Those who didn't complete the packet by the end of the session had to repeat it.

No way would Chad repeat. Thankfully, he thought what the detective had to say was interesting, unlike the majority of the class. She discussed different kinds of offenses. How they could be avoided. Options available to you if you got arrested. How it was better to cooperate with law enforcement.

As Chad sat there, he noticed that most weren't filling out their packets. Some were secretly texting. Others were whispering to each other. And some weren't doing anything at all.

As Chad stared at their faces, he could tell they couldn't care less. They were going to get into trouble again. They didn't think they would get caught.

"Nobody does," the detective stated. And if they did, "the risk would match the reward." This meant they would do it again. And again.

Chad realized he was going down the wrong path with his drinking and isolation. He wasn't able to stop himself. He was happy he'd been caught.

Chapter 60

LOCKER ROOM

Chad thought he would feel great when he stepped back into the locker room. He thought all the familiar sounds and smells might wash away any lingering bad memories. About the accident. About how he'd been annihilated by Dominic Vasquez.

But that didn't happen.

He decided to empty his mind. The best thing for him to do was suit up and get back into the wrestling room.

There were only a few guys inside the locker room. He went over to his locker and started to change for practice.

He took out his shoes and his clothes. He prepped like a robot, trying to keep his mind blank.

It was tough. After closing his locker, he realized all he needed to do was walk to the wrestling room. But he didn't move.

God, it would be so easy to put my clothes back on and sneak out of here. I could swipe a beer. Hide out. Get drunk, he thought. *Snap out of it. That idea sucks.*

"Face this," he said out loud. "Face all of it."

He started moving again.

Before he knew it, he was out of the locker room and on his way to where his life had fallen apart.

It was an accident. It was an accident, he thought as he opened the door to the wrestling room.

Music played. A Mobb Deep song.

Instantly, Chad was transported by the temperature and smell of the room. He felt calmer. He'd been away long enough to recoil at the smell of body odor, well-used wrestling mats, bad breath, and sweaty teenage boys.

The team was busy practicing. Then they saw him. They all stopped.

I'm not that important, he thought. *I need to get over myself.*

Ryan, Amman, Noah, and Tighe smiled as they got back into position.

Everyone seemed to go about their business. Chad stood watching them.

Then his eyes turned to the mat where he'd had his wrestle-off match with Marcus. He stared at the white circle. It was the place where the worst thing ever had happened. The circle burned bright against the red mat.

"Erickson!" Coach Mustain yelled over the music. "Grab a partner."

"I'll do it, Coach." Tighe ran over to Chad. "What's up?"

Tighe held up his hand and Chad grabbed it.

"Are we just going over some moves?" Chad asked.

"Yeah, Coach wants us to focus on fighting off our backs. We've lost four matches because of that weakness."

"Ouch."

As they walked over to an available practice area, Chad realized that he had something to add to the team. He'd always fought well off his back. It was one of the drills he would nag Marcus to practice with him.

"I want to see extra effort, you guys!" Coach Mustain yelled. He was walking up and down the wrestling room.

Chad and Tighe got into position to practice.

What if my loss to Dominic wasn't a fluke? What if I don't have it anymore? Dude, just breathe, he told himself.

"Are you ready?" Tighe asked.

Chad nodded. Tighe didn't give him a second. He shot in and took him straight to the mat.

Chad landed on his back with a thud. The first person he thought about was Marcus.

Instinctively, Chad started to turn himself. He grabbed Tighe's arms so that he couldn't move him into a worse position.

Too slow! Too slow! Chad thought as Tighe maneuvered into a superior position.

Try as he might, Chad couldn't stop Tighe from getting his arm around his neck. Chad was quickly being overpowered.

Out of the corner of his eye, Chad could see Ryan, Amman, Noah, and Coach Mustain watching.

I am being dusted at practice! In a real match, it would already be over. I am never going to get my spot at one seventy back, Chad thought.

He forced himself to block out all of that negativity. He concentrated on his breathing.

He knew he was in a losing position. He'd been there before.

As he held Tighe's arm, he remembered everything he'd been taught.

He knew he just needed to remain calm. Sure, it'd be easier to let Tighe pin him. Then he wouldn't have to wrestle. He could just hang out in his room and—

That wasn't an option. Chad knew it.

He started to use his legs to roll over. Tighe was under him. Tighe's arm loosened around his neck.

Chad seized the moment. He broke loose from Tighe's hold. Then, as Tighe moved to get up, Chad turned and wrapped one arm around Tighe's neck and the other around his leg.

Chad knew what he had to do. He just

had to hold on. He just had to outlast his opponent. Whether that opponent was another person, grief, or himself.

Chad just needed to hold on.

Chapter 61

LESSONS LEARNED

A new person joined the grief support group. His name was Darryl. He had lost his father, just like Angelique.

Angelique and June wanted the new guy to talk more. But he was only giving short answers. Darryl was evasive as he tried to hold back tears.

I wonder where he is in the stages of grief. Denial? Anger? Bargaining? Depression? Acceptance? Sounds like denial to me for sure.

"Nothing matters to me anymore," Darryl finally said in a loud tone. "It was tough taking care of him toward the end. I hated it. But I'd do it again in a heartbeat to have him back."

Darryl started to cry now.

Chad eyed Angelique and June. Angelique wiped tears from her eyes. June stared at Darryl with sadness.

Chad remembered being where Darryl was. Some days he still felt like that. Somehow, though, he knew he'd moved past it. At least a little bit.

"I hated feeling the way you feel," Chad finally said.

"I hate it too," Darryl managed to say.

Chad eyed Angelique. She nodded her head for him to continue.

"I can't tell you when the way you feel now will end." Chad took a deep breath as he felt himself starting to get emotional. "I *can* tell you that it does get easier, losing somebody. You just have to reach a point where you accept how you feel. You have to live your life. You can't hide from the people who care about you. You need them more than you know."

Darryl nodded his head.

Chad eyed Angelique and June. They were both smiling at him. Angelique wiped some tears from her eyes.

Chapter 62

CONTINUING TO HEAL

Chad's heart was beating a mile a minute.

He hid behind a small truck as he watched Maria walk out of her house and make her way to school. Chad pressed himself against the side of the truck as she walked by. He realized he was holding his breath when he heard her footsteps go past him on the other side.

So now I'm a stalker, he thought as he followed her. *Why can't I just talk to her?*

He must have been clomping like a horse because she turned around almost immediately.

"Chad," she said, surprised.

"Hi," he replied, noticing that she wasn't smiling.

"What's up?"

"Can I walk with you?" he asked.

"Okay."

Chad nervously walked over to her. He was shaking. Some alcohol would've calmed his nerves. But he knew now that it wasn't a real cure. Chad understood that speaking with Maria was the only way he would feel better.

"How are you?" Chad asked. Maria stared at the ground.

"Good," Maria replied. Chad thought this conversation would be easier—that Maria would make it easier. "How are your classes?"

God. This is awkward.

"I'm doing okay. You?" she replied.

"My classes are fine. That's the one

thing I haven't actually messed up." He looked at Maria with hope.

Maria stared at Chad. He could feel himself getting more nervous. Opening up. Being in touch with his feelings. It was still new to him. Which was why he knew he had to keep talking.

"Maria." He took her hand. She stopped walking. "I'm *so* sorry. I've been a jerk. I've treated you so bad. I was just hurting so much because of what happened with Marcus. I was blaming myself. I'm so sorry. I'm so scared right now that you'll—"

"Chad." Her voice stopped his fusillade of words. "I understand. I just wanted you to talk to me. I wanted to be there for you. I still do."

She smiled at him. His heart was pounding. He felt his eyes welling up with tears. He leaned in and they kissed. It was warm and special. It was everything that Chad needed.

After what happened with Marcus, he knew he needed Maria. But he was in a punishing mood then. He didn't feel like he deserved anything that might make him feel okay. Make him feel good about himself.

As they stood on the sidewalk together, Maria gave Chad the loving hug that he needed. It was a welcome-home hug. The kind that would greet someone after a long journey. Even though he hadn't gone any-where physically.

But mentally? He'd been to hell and back.

Chapter 63

NOWHERE TO HIDE

The bleachers on both sides of the Guerin High School gym were packed. Students, faculty, and family from Guerin and Shepard were cheering for their team as they battled it out on the mat.

Shepard was having a bad night. So far, all of their wrestlers had lost. Amman was up. Chad eyed his friend as he walked over to the waiting area. He was next once Amman's match was done.

He would compete for Shepard High School at one hundred seventy pounds.

His best weight. The spot he wanted so badly. Again, he would be facing Dominic Vasquez. The wrestler who had demolished Chad the last time he was in this gym. The last time he competed.

Chad blocked the thought from his mind.

As Amman's match started, Chad turned and grabbed a jump rope. He started jumping.

Focus breathing. In and out. Jump. Jump. Jump. Nice and slow.

He heard a loud thud on the mat. The crowd roared.

Chad turned and saw Amman on his back.

For a split second, Chad saw himself lift Marcus up, then slam him to the mat in the wrestling room.

He shook the image from his head. He knew he couldn't think about that now. Instead, he looked up in the stands. Chad saw his parents. They were talking to each other. Maria was sitting next to them. She waved at Chad. He smiled.

Chad knew that was just what he needed. He wished he could leave right now with his girl. But he knew he had to wrestle. Chad wanted to face Dominic again. He wanted to know for sure where he stood.

He glanced at Maria again. Someone caught his eye. It was Debbie. She was sitting next to Maria with Mike Solomon. Chad didn't recognize Debbie at first because she'd colored her hair. It was darker than before.

He stared at Debbie and Mike sitting together. Mike was a decent guy. Debbie and Maria were best friends. Chad cared for Maria a lot. He didn't want to do anything to get in the way of their friendship. But Mike wasn't Marcus.

He heard another thud. Then he heard

three quick hand slaps on the mat. Chad didn't have to turn around to know that Amman had been pinned. The cheers from the Guerin High School fans told him all he needed to know.

Guerin was wiping the floor with Shepard. And Chad knew that Dominic Vasquez did not want to break the streak.

Chapter 64

TRIAL BY FIRE

Chad couldn't believe it. Marcus's family was there. He saw them as he walked out to meet Dominic in the center mat.

Even though Chad talked with Dave, he still couldn't help wondering if the Pagels were there to see him lose. Seeing him get wiped out might make them feel better about what he'd done to their son.

Chad clenched his fists and closed his eyes. He knew if he had any shot at continuing wrestling. If he had any wrestling scholarship in his future. He would have to block out all negative thoughts.

Chad and Dominic shook hands. Dominic's grip was extra firm. Like he was letting Chad know he intended to win this match just like the last time.

He eyed Coach Mustain as he got into a crouching position. Coach smiled confidently at Chad. He knew Chad could beat Dominic Vasquez.

Chad knew his problem. His own thoughts would bring him down.

He started to think about that day in the wrestling room with Marcus …

The whistle blew.

Dominic made a fast move and grabbed Chad. Chad held his ground as they grappled. Dominic was strong, and he easily turned Chad in a half-circle. Chad lifted up his foot. It skidded on the mat.

Suddenly, Dominic used all his strength to lift Chad up and slam him down. In a split second, he was on top of Chad, who had rolled onto his back.

Chad figured everybody was worried about him now.

Coach Mustain wasn't smiling. His parents were probably hoping the match would be over fast. Maria was probably crying. His teammates were probably disappointed.

Chad wondered if he could recover. Was this payback for what happened to Marcus?

Don't think. Just breathe.

He knew he was in a bad spot. Being on his back was not ideal. But he'd been there before. And he'd gotten out of it.

Chad was surprised by Dominic's eagerness. He was going directly for the pin. He probably thought he could wipe the mat with Chad. He did a few months before.

But now?

Chad could feel Dominic's body tense up as he started to move slowly. He didn't get far. But Dominic was going to have expend a lot of energy if he hoped to keep him in one spot.

"Come on, Dominic!" he heard people yell. "Take him out like last time!"

Chad tried to stay calm. Having Dominic's weight on him wasn't making it easy.

Chad slowly maneuvered his body. Dominic probably didn't realize what was happening. But Chad was moving himself out of his opponent's hold.

Dominic tried to keep him in place, but it wasn't working.

Chad noticed that Dominic's heart was pounding. He was weaker and out of breath. Chad was still fresh despite being taken down.

Chad was all instinct now. He pressed up as hard as he could. He moved out from under Dominic. At the same time, he slammed Dominic on his back.

Chad froze. He had slammed Dominic with the same ferocity that he had slammed Marcus.

Before Chad overthought the move, he brought his arm under Dominic's neck. Then he reached under his leg and latched his hands together.

It had taken a lot of muscle to get himself out of Dominic's hold, then get him on his back.

Pinning him in this position was going to require even more strength.

"One!" he heard the referee yell.

Chad started to get nervous.

Really nervous.

Dominic wasn't pushing hard. He wasn't fighting like crazy to get out of the pin. Chad thought he really hurt him, just like he'd hurt Marcus.

"Two!"

Then Dominic gave a ferocious push. He wanted out of the hold. Chad closed his eyes and held his move.

He was so close. So close to redemption. So close to triumph.

"Three!"

Guerin High School's side of the gym roared with disappointment.

Chad stood up and extended his hand. Dominic took it and Chad helped him up.

"Good match, man," Dominic said. "I thought I had you."

"Thanks," Chad said. "You too."

As Chad walked away, he burst into tears. With this victory, he knew he was going to be okay. He knew he was meant to wrestle. Meant to have a normal life.

He thought about covering his face with a towel. But right now the normally reserved Chad Erickson didn't care who saw him cry.

Chad walked over to his team. He was greeted with a bear hug from Coach Mustain and high fives from his teammates.

"There are still more matches, boys." Coach Mustain smiled. "Let's hope Chad's victory sets a new tone. We're in it to win it. Let's go, Shepard!"

Chad saw his parents and Maria. They were standing a few feet away. There were hugs all around. His mom was crying. His dad had tears in his eyes.

"We're so proud of you, Chad," he said in a soft voice.

Then he looked up and saw Marcus's family. He went over to them.

"I'm sorry ..." he choked out.

Before the words were out of his mouth, Marcus's parents embraced him.

"Hey, stranger," Marcus's dad said. "That was a great match."

"We've missed you, Chad. Marcus

would have been proud," his mom said, her lips quivering.

Dave gave Chad a hug.

"You wiped the mat with that guy. It was rad!" Dave's eyes were beaming as he spoke. Chad just smiled as the tears of happiness continued.

Chapter 65

ACCEPTANCE

Chad wiped a tear from his cheek as he straightened up some flowers near Marcus's headstone.

He hadn't expected to ever feel okay in the cemetery. He wasn't excited to be there. But he didn't feel like he needed to hide from it anymore.

"We gotta keep this place looking nice," Chad said out loud. It helped him stay present if he talked to Marcus as if he could hear him. "We can't let people know what a slob you really are."

Chad thought about what had happened. Marcus dying.

Shutting down. Closing out his parents. Maria. Everything and everyone who meant anything to him.

He started drinking.

Shoplifting.

Getting arrested.

Standing before a judge.

Attending the grief support group.

Being lost.

Finding himself again.

Making things right with the people who cared about him.

Beating Dominic Vasquez when nobody thought he could.

Most importantly, Chad Erickson had come back from all the hurt of Marcus's death. He still had his bad days. But overall, he was doing okay.

Chad was hanging out with his parents again. He and Maria were back on track.

He even tolerated hanging out with Debbie and Mike. Sometimes.

Plus, he was making weekly visits to Marcus's parents' house. That made him feel especially good. Marcus's mother told him that Marcus died from a heart defect. There was nothing anyone could do.

He would talk with Marcus's parents about school. About funny things he remembered about Marcus. About his college dreams. But he mainly spent time with Dave. They would work out in the garage. He showed Dave some wrestling moves. The kid was going to try out for Shepard's team next year.

"You probably knew Coach Mustain was going to do what he did." Chad stared at Marcus's tombstone. He didn't want to smile, but he didn't think Marcus would mind.

Chad missed a lot of the wrestling season. After the match with Guerin, there were only a few more meets. He won them all, but the season was essentially over. As far as he knew, no college recruiters had scouted him.

He started focusing on going to a community college. His plan was to transfer in two years to whatever wrestling school would take him.

Then one afternoon while he was studying, the phone rang. It was a scout from Arizona State University.

Apparently, Coach Mustain had sent them a YouTube link of Chad's victory over Dominic Vasquez.

ASU was interested in Chad. Coach helped him put together a DVD of his best wins. Chad was confident something good would happen.

He wasn't supposed to be going off to college alone. Marcus was supposed to go too. Maybe not to the same schools. But at least share the experience. Like best friends do. Chad felt a wave of sadness sweep over him.

Marcus would be happy for him. What happened to him was a tragedy. Chad needed to make the most of his life. And Marcus would be the first person to say so.

"You're always with me," Chad said in a shaky voice. "You haven't gone anywhere. We'll be reunited one day. And you'll probably kick my butt on the mat. Maybe."

Chad couldn't help but cry. He gently wiped more tears from his eyes. As he did, he read the inscription on Marcus's gravestone.

Marcus Pagel
He made us laugh.
He was loved by all.
He left us too soon.
He will be missed.
1998–2015

Chad took a photo out of his pocket. It was a copy of the one of Marcus and him when they were in kindergarten. It was taken on the day they first met.

Chad still couldn't believe that Marcus was gone. It didn't feel right. He knew it didn't have to. He knew it never would. He just had to accept it.

And he had.

Chad put the picture on the grave. Then he sat back and continued talking to his best friend.

WANT TO KEEP READING?...

Turn the page for a sneak peek at another book from the Gravel Road series: Evan Jacobs's *Self. Destructed.*

ISBN: 978-1-62250-722-1

Ashley

Nice shirt." Ashley Walters smiled as she passed Michael Ellis. She was paying a compliment to his T-shirt for the band the Who. It was the one where the *O* in the name had an arrow coming out of it, and there was a red, white, and blue bull's-eye behind it.

"You want it?" Michael replied looking up from his *MacWorld* magazine. Ashley laughed. Her smile was enough to let him know she thought he was okay; that he could keep talking to her.

"I'll give it to you, seriously." Michael

started to lift his shirt up, ignoring the fact that he was wearing a jacket. Realizing it would be impossible to take off, Michael stopped trying.

"Come on, keep going." Ashley's smile became a stern expression. "You *did* offer."

Michael stared at her. Ashley had really inviting hazel eyes. They went well with her dark complexion and thick brown hair. She wore a pair of white tennis shoes, white shorts, and a red T-shirt.

"Okay, I'll let you off the hook." She smiled. "I can see by your jacket that you run for the school. Running's cool."

"You like to run?" Michael asked.

Ashley nodded her head.

"You want to run together sometime?" He asked the question before he realized what he was saying.

"You think you can keep up with me?" She jogged in place. "I'm pretty fast."

"I run the hundred-yard dash."

CHAPTER 1

"Wow, that's a humble brag." She smiled.

Michael liked how she teased him and seemed interested at the same time.

"You're new here," Michael stated.

"Do I stand out that much?"

"In a good way."

Michael had no idea why he was saying all these things. There was something about Ashley. He felt drawn to her. She didn't seem like the other girls at Willmore High School. He felt like it was okay to talk with her like this.

"Well, I've gotta run. Not literally." She smiled again. Dazzling. "But you better stay in training. Especially if you're gonna keep up when you take me running."

"Okay."

"I'm Ashley."

"Michael."

He wanted to set up a time for their run but she was gone.

Michael thought about going after her but he didn't. He had a feeling he would be talking to her again. He just didn't know when, which kind of bothered him.

John walked up. He was wearing the same Willmore High School track jacket that Michael was wearing. It said Willmore across the back and had a runner in the center.

"Who was that girl you were talking to?" John asked.

"That was Ashley."

"She's cute."

Michael continued to watch Ashley as she walked away. Eventually, she blended into the crowd of students.

The school year had basically just started, and Michael thought it was gonna be a great one.